A CHRISTMAS BABY AT ROOKERY HOUSE

ROSIE HENDRY

A Christmas Baby at Rookery House

Copyright © 2023 by Rosie Hendry
ISBN: 978-1-914443-27-5

Published by Rookery House Press
Cover design by designforwriters.com

For Olivia

CHAPTER 1

Sunday 5th October 1941 – Rookery House, Norfolk

Marianne Fordham stood by her bedroom window staring out at the moonlit garden, thinking how she'd always used to love a full moon. But not any more. The moon wasn't just a clotted cream coloured orb sailing high across the night sky, bathing the world in its pale ghostly light and changing the colours of day into shades of monochrome. Now, a full moon brought potential danger to her husband and even more worry to Marianne.

Somewhere up there, Alex was flying towards tonight's ops target. Perhaps he'd even been piloting one of the aeroplanes she'd heard droning overhead earlier. The darkness which normally gave him, and other airmen like him, some protection was gone tonight. What was so blithely known now as a *bomber's moon* might show up their targets more clearly, but it also left planes more visible and vulnerable to attack from enemy fire.

Marianne sighed, biting her bottom lip to hold back tears. She felt so helpless. There wasn't a thing she could do to help him, to keep him safe. All she could do was hope that he'd return safely to his base in Lincolnshire sometime in the early hours of the morning. Waiting, hoping and worrying about him was hard. It often left her unable to sleep.

Leaving the blackout curtain slightly open so the pale moonlight dimly lit the room, Marianne went over to check on her daughter, Emily, who was sound asleep in her cot. The little girl was sleeping in the position she usually moved into during the night – kneeling face down, with her head, shoulders and arms on the mattress and her bottom in the air. Marianne adjusted the soft covers over her daughter and gently kissed her head. Emily had no trouble sleeping, but then she had no idea of the danger her father faced whenever he flew on ops. Marianne hoped her daughter would never experience that worry and by the time Emily was old enough to have some understanding of what was going on, the war would long be over, and they could all be living together as a family.

A sharp kick on the inside of her enlarged belly made Marianne gasp. She placed a hand on her stomach and stroked her dressing gown over where she'd felt it. The sensation of a kick or elbow jabbing inside her was a strange feeling, reminding Marianne that her and Alex's unborn child was very much alive and growing. Within a few months, it would, all being well, be born around Christmas time and be another welcome addition to their family. Perhaps her wakefulness was affecting it, Marianne wondered.

She decided to go downstairs and make herself some hot milk in the hope it would help her sleep. Tomorrow was going to be a busy day with another Make and Mend party on at the village hall where she'd be teaching some more sewing skills.

Marianne might be blooming at this stage in her pregnancy, but she still must get enough rest for her own sake, the baby's and to keep up with Emily who was so full of energy.

Downstairs in the kitchen, the range was sending out a welcome warmth as it had been stoked up as usual before bed. Marianne fetched the jug of milk from the cold marble slab in the pantry and was pouring some into a small saucepan to heat up, when the doorway from the hall opened and Hettie appeared, carrying a holder with a lit candle.

'I wondered who it was.' Hettie came in and closed the door quietly behind her, then put her holder on the table, adding another warm yellow glow of light besides the candle that Marianne had brought down with her. 'Couldn't you sleep?'

'No. I thought some hot milk might help. Would you like some?' Marianne offered.

'Yes please.' Hettie opened the door into the firebox of the range and added some more wood from the log basket nearby.

Marianne poured some more milk into the saucepan. 'I hope I didn't wake you coming downstairs.'

'No, you didn't,' Hettie reassured her as she closed the range door again. 'I've been awake for a while. Thinking things over as you do in the middle of the night.' She gave a knowing smile.

Marianne put the saucepan onto the hot plate and then returned the milk jug to the pantry. Back in the kitchen she stood by the range watching the milk to make sure it didn't boil over, while Hettie took two cups from a dresser and placed them ready on the table.

'What was keeping you awake?' Hettie asked, coming to stand by the range alongside Marianne. 'Is Emily all right?'

'She's fine, fast asleep with her bottom in the air. You know how she likes to sleep that way.'

Hettie gave a laugh. 'She must be comfortable, though I don't think I would be sleeping in that position, but then her bones are a lot younger than mine!' She fixed her gaze on Marianne's face, her eyes concerned behind her round glasses. 'Why weren't you asleep too?'

Marianne stared into the saucepan of milk for a moment before raising her eyes to meet Hettie's. She considered making up some excuse but knew it was no good pretending. Hettie was shrewd enough to suspect when someone wasn't telling the truth.

'I was worrying about Alex,' Marianne said flatly. 'I know he's often up there flying on ops, but when it's a full moon…' She gestured upwards with her hands. 'It just feels even worse than usual because it's easier for his plane to be seen. The whole point of being protected by going on ops under cover of darkness is gone!' Her voice rose as her chest tightened.

Hettie took a step closer and put her hand on Marianne's arm. 'I understand, but you should try not to fret. There's nothing you can do to help Alex and getting yourself worked up about it isn't going to do you any good, or the baby.'

Marianne's eyes filled with tears. 'But that's like telling a river to flow up a hill. I worry about Alex because I love him, and I'm scared of what might happen to him. Flying planes over enemy territory is so *dangerous*. I know what happens to many of the men who do it and I…' Her voice cracked, and she couldn't stop her tears spilling over and running down her face.

Hettie moved the saucepan of milk off the hot plate to the side of the range, then took hold of Marianne's arm and steered her towards the table, pulling out a chair for her to sit down.

'You sit there, and I'll sort the hot milk out. Then we can

talk about this.' Hettie fished a clean white handkerchief out of her dressing gown pocket and handed it to Marianne.

'Thank you.' Marianne took the soft handkerchief and used it to wipe the tears from her face. While Hettie busied herself with their hot drink, Marianne focused on bringing her emotions under control. Crying would not help Alex, she told herself firmly.

'Here, this will help. I've added a bit of nutmeg as well,' Hettie said a short while later as she placed a cup in front of Marianne and then sat down beside her. 'How are you feeling?'

Marianne sniffed. 'Silly. I'm not usually so tearful, it's just…'

'You're expecting a baby. That often makes women more emotional.' Hettie put her hand on Marianne's arm. 'Having a husband flying ops doesn't help either.'

Marianne shook her head. 'It doesn't. There was a time when I never thought I'd be married to Alex. Even seeing him again seemed like an impossibility.'

She recalled how when she'd first come to Rookery House as an expectant mother, Alex hadn't even known she was expecting his child and she had mistakenly believed he was engaged to someone else. Fate had brought them together again and misunderstandings had been uncovered, resolved and they'd married when Emily was a couple of months old. Since then, the Royal Air Force had ruled their lives while Alex had completed his pilot training and they'd had few chances to spend time together. Now he was a qualified bomber pilot, operational and still under the thumb of the Air Force. Despite not seeing much of her husband, Marianne's marriage to him was precious to her. She wanted nothing to change that.

'I don't want to lose him.' Marianne's voice came out in a

croak, tears filling her eyes and threatening to spill over once more.

'I hope you never do,' Hettie said, her blue eyes sympathetic. 'It was a wonderful day when you two finally sorted things out between you and decided to get married. It was a lovely thing to happen for you both and for Emily, too.'

'What can I do?' Marianne asked, grabbing hold of Hettie's hand. 'It's so hard worrying if he's safe. If he'll come back. I know so many wives and mothers are going through the same thing. I'm not the only one. How do they cope with it?'

'The best way to deal with worries like this is to keep yourself busy during the day,' Hettie said sagely. 'It will give you less time to dwell on things and worry about the maybes and mights, as well as tiring you out so you'll sleep better at night. In my experience, worrying is a waste of energy because *most* things don't happen. But then I've not had a husband in wartime, or any other time come to that!' Hettie gave a rueful smile. 'But I *have* worried enough about things over the years and, looking back, it didn't help me. Only got me into a pickle and took up energy that could have been better spent elsewhere.' She gave Marianne's hand a gentle squeeze. 'Keep yourself occupied. There's the Make and Mend party tomorrow afternoon and you'll be even busier when this one's born.' She nodded towards Marianne's rounded belly.

'You're right,' Marianne agreed.

'I'm always here to talk to whenever you want,' Hettie offered. 'Just take things one day at a time. Alex wouldn't want you getting worried and upset, would he?'

Marianne shook her head. 'No. He doesn't even tell me about what he does when I ask. He always prefers to talk about other things when we speak on the telephone.'

'He's right and I'm sure that helps him by focusing on the nicer side of life.' Hettie nodded towards Marianne's cup.

'Drink that up before it goes cold, then you can go back to bed and get some sleep.'

Marianne did as she was told and took a long drink of the warm milk, which had a delicious sweet spicy taste of nutmeg. It was soothing, and she felt herself begin to relax. 'Tastes good.'

Hettie put down her cup on the table after having a mouthful of her own hot milk. 'It will help us both sleep.'

'Talking to you has helped, too. Thank you, Hettie.' Marianne gave the older woman a tentative smile. 'It's put things into perspective. I'll do my best to remember what you said and keep myself busy.'

But whatever she did, Marianne knew that the worry wouldn't completely leave her, not while Alex was still risking his life flying on ops. She wished with all her heart that this awful war was over, Alex was safe, and they could all live together in peace.

CHAPTER 2

Genevieve Hamilton-Jones, otherwise known as Evie Jones, tiptoed down the stairs at Rookery House a little after half past six the next morning. Wearing the blue linen dress of her Voluntary Aid Detachment nurse's uniform, she was ready for some breakfast, before heading off to start her shift at Great Plumstead Hall Hospital.

'Good morning,' Evie greeted Hettie as she went into the kitchen. As usual, the older woman was up first and stood by the range, stirring a saucepan of porridge.

Hettie gave her a welcoming smile. 'Morning! It's looking like a lovely day out there today, blue sky and sunshine. We've got to make the most of the good days now we're into autumn. Do you want some porridge?'

'Yes, please.' Evie took a bowl from the table and carried it over to the range, where Hettie spooned out a steaming helping of creamy porridge for her.

'There's some stewed spiced plums to go with it if you like.' Hettie pointed to the dish of cooked, dark pink fruit standing on the table.

'Thank you.' Evie put her hand in her dress pocket and brought out an envelope. 'Would you post this in the village for me, please? I've stuck a stamp on it already.'

'Of course, I will.' Hettie took the envelope and glanced at the name and address on the front. 'Another one for Private Blythe?'

Evie nodded and gave the older woman a wry smile. Hettie was still in the habit of referring to Evie's friend as *Private Blythe*. But now he was just plain Mr Ned Blythe, having lost his rank when he'd been medically discharged from the army after leaving Great Plumstead Hall Hospital. Ned hadn't been bothered to see it go and was relieved not to have to return to the battlefield.

'I think it's lovely how you've kept in touch with him, especially after all the worry you had with him when he was a patient at the hospital.' Hettie put the letter in the pocket of her crossover blue paisley print apron.

'Ned's a fine letter writer and I enjoy our correspondence. He's a good man. I like him.'

Hettie raised her eyebrows, her blue eyes twinkling in amusement as they met Evie's.

'But not like that, Hettie!' Evie rolled her eyes. 'We're just friends who share a passion for books and that's what we mostly talk about in our letters. My ghastly experience of being married to Douglas has put me off *ever* getting involved in a relationship with anyone again.'

'Fair enough, I didn't mean to pry.' Hettie looked apologetic.

'It's fine. I've nothing to hide about my friendship with Ned.' Evie gave her a reassuring smile. 'I'd better eat my breakfast. I don't want to be late, or Matron Reed will be on the warpath!'

Evie sat down at the table, poured herself a cup of tea from the teapot, then helped herself to some plums, enjoying the delicious combination of sweetness and spice and how it complemented the creaminess of porridge. As she ate, her mind drifted back to January when Ned had arrived at Great Plumstead Hall Hospital. His eyes had been injured in a battle and were swathed in bandages. When Evie'd changed his dressings for the first time, she'd recognised the V-shaped nick in his ear just above his earlobe. She recalled how her heart had plummeted when she had realised that this man had known her before in the life she'd fled from.

Private Blythe had been the chauffeur to Evie's husband's parents and had often driven her and Douglas around. Evie had been terrified that if his sight returned, he'd recognise her and reveal her identity, putting her in danger once more. Evie's husband had been cruel and abusive towards her and she'd taken the drastic step of faking her own death to escape from him.

Starting again at Rookery House and working at Great Plumstead Hall Hospital had given her a chance of freedom and safety. Everything had been going well until Private Blythe arrived. Thankfully, when his sight did return he hadn't given her away and they'd formed an unlikely friendship over their mutual love of books. Through Private Blythe, Evie had eventually found out that Douglas had been killed in action and that she was finally free.

Evie had almost finished eating when Flo, her roommate who worked as a Land Girl here at Rookery House, came into the kitchen. She was closely followed by Thea. Each of them said a cheery good morning, helped themselves to porridge and plums and were soon seated at the table, along with Hettie, tucking into their breakfast.

'Is everything ready for Violet?' Hettie asked, directing her question to Thea.

'Almost. I'll change the sheets on my bed after breakfast and make up the camp bed for myself in the dining room later,' Thea explained.

'What time is Violet arriving?' Flo asked, scooping up a spoonful of porridge.

'She should be on the half past one train.' Thea's face lit up. 'I'm really looking forward to having Violet staying. I hope she'll take the chance to rest properly and recuperate while she's here as her job as station officer is a heavy responsibility.'

'It will be a big change here from London,' Evie said. 'It took me a while to get used to the quiet, but I love it now.' She glanced at her watch. 'I must go.' She stood up, put her empty bowl and cup by the sink and headed upstairs to finish getting ready for work.

Evie rode her bicycle across the wide sweep of gravel in front of the Great Plumstead Hall Hospital and headed for the enclosed courtyard at the rear. She bumped over the cobbles towards the old stables where staff stored their bicycles, and after leaving her bike in there, headed in through the back door and made her way to the cloakroom to hang up her coat and put on the rest of her uniform.

Opening the door of the cloakroom, she saw her friend and fellow VAD nurse Hazel Robertson was already in there along with another young woman who Evie hadn't met before. Hazel was helping the young woman put on her nurse's white veil head covering over her blonde hair.

'Morning Evie,' Hazel greeted her cheerfully. 'Delia, this is Evie Jones. Evie, Delia's our new VAD who's starting work here today.'

The new arrival held out her hand, a friendly smile on her

face. 'Pleased to meet you, Evie. I'm Cordelia Hastings, but please call me Delia.'

Evie shook her hand. 'Good to meet you, Delia. Welcome to Great Plumstead Hall. Which hospital were you at before?'

'Oh, nowhere!' Delia giggled, her blue eyes dancing. 'This is my *first* placement and I'm so excited to be starting nursing properly at last. I've *always* wanted to be a nurse. It took me *ages* to convince my parents I could do this. Father's a friend of Lord Campbell-Gryce, so they finally relented as I could work and live here,' Delia explained. 'And here I am!'

'There, that should hold now.' Hazel pushed the final hairpin into place and made a last tweak of Delia's veil.

'Thank you.' Delia checked her reflection in the mirror, turning her head from side to side. 'Why do we have to wear veils that are so difficult to put on?'

Hazel and Evie both looked at each other and then laughed.

'We *all* say exactly the same thing when we first start,' Evie said as she put on her clean white apron, with its red cross on the chest, over her blue dress. 'You'll soon get used to it and be able to do your own.'

'I'm to take you to Miss Howlett, the hospital secretary,' Hazel told Delia. 'She'll show you around and introduce you to everyone before you start work. If you come with me.' She opened the door and motioned for Delia to go through it. 'I'll see you at the briefing, Evie.'

Left alone, Evie finished putting on the rest of her uniform, her white arm cuffs and then her veil. As she carefully pinned the material on her head, she recalled her own first day here. Like Delia, Hazel had helped Evie with her veil, folding the fabric into neat pleats and then pinning them into place. It was tricky to do properly, and that day Evie's hands had been all fingers and thumbs with nerves, so she'd been grateful for the assistance. That was almost a year ago, and now Evie was happily settled and enjoyed working here, and she and Hazel had become good friends.

Evie checked her reflection in the mirror, making sure the red cross on the front of her veil was positioned in the centre of her forehead, as she didn't want to give Matron Reed anything to complain about. Then, leaving the cloakroom, she headed for the nurses' sitting room for the briefing, which happened at the start of each shift.

'Delia seems nice,' Evie said to Hazel while they waited for Matron to arrive. They were gathered with the other VADs, some going on duty like them, and others at the end of their shift. The briefing was an important part of their day, keeping staff informed of what was happening on the wards and with patients.

'She's very enthusiastic about being a VAD but hasn't got any proper experience yet. Only her first aid, home nursing and hygiene courses and a bit of voluntary work,' Hazel said in a low voice. 'Not having worked in a hospital before, she's bound to feel like she's being thrown into the deep end here. I...' She halted as the door opened and Matron Reed marched in, her immaculate uniform dress straining over her portly frame.

Evie was aware of the instant change of atmosphere in the room, the way each nurse stood as if to attention, their relaxed moods evaporating. Everyone here had been on the receiving end of Matron's wrath and knew better than to give her any cause for complaint.

'Good morning.' Matron Reed's shrewd brown eyes passed slowly over each of them, assessing their appearance, checking their uniforms were spotless and being worn correctly. As Matron's eyes fell on her, Evie felt herself tense further. She should be used to this by now, but the woman could be so fearsome. Evie still felt on tenterhooks each time she came under Matron Reed's scrutiny. Thankfully, Matron's gaze moved on without comment.

'It's been a quiet night,' Matron said in her soft Scottish accent as she began the briefing. 'We have two patients being discharged today and as yet, I have had no news of more to take their place, but we know there will certainly be more. Nurse Robertson and Nurse Jones, I want you on dressings this morning…' Matron continued with the list of jobs, giving each nurse plenty to do. Then, with a curt nod of her head, she swivelled round lightly on the balls of her feet and strode out.

As soon as the door closed behind her, the atmosphere in the room lifted.

'Let's get to it,' Hazel said. 'Shall we start on Library Ward?'

Evie nodded. 'That's fine by me.' She leaned closer to her friend as they headed for the door. 'I'm glad Matron didn't have any complaints about anyone this morning.'

'It's early yet.' Hazel gave a wry smile, holding the door open for Evie. 'There are plenty of hours left in the shift for her to find fault.'

Evie rolled her eyes and the pair of them laughed as they headed off to the storeroom to prepare their dressings trolleys.

CHAPTER 3

'Welcome to Rookery House!' Thea threw her arm wide as they reached the gateway of her home after walking back from Great Plumstead station. 'What do you think?'

Violet cocked her head to one side as she looked at the Victorian built red brick house, her shrewd brown eyes taking it in behind her owlish horn-rimmed spectacles. 'I think it's delightful! And just as you described to me.' Her gaze met Thea's and she gave a wide smile. 'I can see why you love it so much. And always have for as long as I've known you, even when you didn't own it!'

Thea laughed, recalling how she'd told Violet about Rookery House when they'd worked as ambulance drivers in France during the Great War. 'I always dreamed I would one day though, and sometimes dreams do come true.' Thea looked at her home and, not for the first time since she'd bought it and moved in back in the summer of 1939, reminded herself how fortunate she was to now live in the house she had loved from an early age. 'Come on, let's get you settled in, and then I can show you around properly.'

'Thank you. It's going to be lovely to stay here for a week. Such a treat.'

'I hope you'll be able to relax here.'

'I'm sure I will. I must admit I feel better already. Being out in the countryside always fills me with happiness,' Violet said.

'Good.' Thea linked her arm through her friend's. 'This way, we go in through the back door.'

'I can't take your bedroom!' Violet declared turning around to look at Thea, a concerned expression on her face. 'Where are you going to sleep?'

'Don't worry about me. I'll be perfectly fine downstairs in the dining room. Although George and Betty, my young evacuees, thought I should put the camp bed in their room! But I'd rather sleep downstairs, so they're not disturbed by me going to bed later or getting up earlier than them.' Thea put Violet's brown leather case down on the bed. 'I *want* you to stay in here,' Thea said firmly. 'It's comfortable and you can get a good night's rest.'

She was happy to loan her bedroom, determined to give Violet a week of rest and recuperation after all she'd been through during the Blitz. When Thea had met Violet at the station, she'd thought her friend looked pale, tired and in dire need of a holiday.

'It is a lovely room.' Violet gazed around the spotlessly clean and tidy bedroom that smelled of lavender and beeswax polish, taking in the colourful patchwork cover on the bed, the matching oak chest of drawers and wardrobe, and the window that looked out from the front of the house over to the field on the opposite side of the road. 'If you're absolutely sure, then I know I'll be most comfortable in here, thank you.'

Thea gave a nod of satisfaction. 'Good, that's settled then. I've cleared out a couple of drawers for you to put your things in and there's space in the wardrobe if you want to hang anything up.'

'It's a long way from our accommodation in France.' Violet gave a wry smile. 'We got through it though, didn't we, with good cheer and the best of friends?'

'We did.' Thea could still picture the room they'd shared in France; it was freezing cold in winter but had served as a refuge for them after their often harrowing days at work driving injured soldiers to hospital. 'And now you're the station officer of an ambulance station! Who'd've thought back then that Violet Steele, breaker of rules, would end up in such a job?'

Violet arched an eyebrow. 'Don't they say former poachers make the best gamekeepers, as they know all the tricks?' she said with a mischievous twinkle in her eye. 'My own experience helps me keep one step ahead of my crews.'

'Does your crew know about your dubious record of rule keeping?' Thea asked.

'Definitely not! Or I'd never hear the end of it from some of them. Imagine if Winnie knew how much I was like her.' She gave a mock shudder. 'It's best for everyone at Station 75 if I maintain my air of sticking to the rules.'

'They're very lucky to have you as their station officer.'

'I count myself fortunate to have such a wonderful crew. All such different individuals, but together they make an incredible team. I hope they'll be all right this week under Winnie's deputy command.' Violet looked uncertain for a moment, but then her face broke into a smile. 'I'm on holiday. I shouldn't be thinking about work, should I?'

'No, but I'll let you off this time.' Thea's voice had a hint of laughter in it. 'From now on, you need to forget about Station

75 and focus on just being yourself and having an enjoyable time.'

'Oh, I intend to, Thea. I've wanted to visit you and Rookery House for so long. Now I'm here, I'm not going to waste a second of it.' Violet took a deep breath and let it out in a long sigh, her shoulders dropping. 'Let my holiday truly begin!'

CHAPTER 4

Like most days on duty at Great Plumstead Hall Hospital, the morning had flown by, Evie thought as she headed to the sluice. She liked to be busy and, with almost all the beds full, there was plenty to keep the staff occupied. They were stretched to get everything done if she was honest, as more than the usual number of the patients were bed-bound in Dining Room Ward, so required more nursing assistance than those men who were mobile.

Carrying a used bed pan into the sluice, she saw that Delia was still doing the same job she'd been given by Matron earlier after being shown around by Miss Howlett – scouring and sterilising bed pans.

As Delia turned around from the sink Evie was shocked at the young woman's reddened tear-stained face.

'Whatever's wrong?' Evie asked. 'Have you scalded yourself with the hot water?'

'No.' Delia sniffed, her chin trembling as her blue eyes filled with tears. 'This wasn't what I thought I'd be doing working as a VAD. I haven't even been *near* a patient! Matron

Reed sent me straight to work in here. When she came in to check on me earlier, I asked if I could go on the ward, but she said *not yet!*' Her voice wavered. 'I asked when that would be, and she told me that *she* would be the judge of that and that I should stop fussing and get on with my work.'

'Matron starts *every* new nurse off in here. It's like she's testing each person out. I started in here and so did Hazel and we both had *months* of experience working on the wards in other hospitals.' Evie put her hand on Delia's shoulder. 'It might not be a nice job, but it's an essential one. Remember, many of the jobs us nurses must do aren't pleasant.'

'This was your first job? Even though you'd already worked in a hospital for months?' Delia echoed, her eyes wide.

Evie nodded. 'Yes.'

'How long were you in here before you got to nurse patients?' Delia asked, her face brightening. 'Do you think I'll be allowed onto the ward working with them tomorrow?'

'To be honest, no. If Matron's satisfied you can do this job properly, you'll then get moved on to cleaning something else.' Evie lowered her voice. 'I'd advise you not to keep asking Matron to move or how long you will be in here, either. Otherwise, you may be stuck in the sluice far longer than you need to be.'

'I didn't expect it to be like this. I thought when I volunteered that I'd be taking patients' temperatures, mopping fevered brows, sitting at their bedside talking to them…' Delia's voice drifted off dreamily before her expression hardened. 'Not this!' She slapped her reddened hand on the side of the large stone sink. 'I'm not sure I can *stand* doing this for much longer.'

Evie nodded sympathetically. She'd hated doing this job herself when she'd first arrived here. 'I'm afraid the only way you're going to be allowed to take any patient's temperature in this hospital is by carrying on doing this job first. If you don't, then your days as a VAD are going to be cut short. I know it's not easy, Delia, but if you persevere, then you *will* get there. Do you think you can try?'

Delia sniffed, blinking away more tears. 'If it's the only way, then I *must*. If I give up and go home, I'll only have Mummy saying she *told* me nursing wasn't right for me.' She raised her chin. 'I am not letting that happen.'

'Good. You can do this,' Evie said in an encouraging voice. 'We all survived and got through it, and so will you.'

Delia straightened her shoulders. 'Thank you, Evie. I appreciate your encouragement and will persevere. I will *not* give up.'

The door of the sluice opened, and Hazel came in. She took one look at Delia and said in a cheery voice. 'It's almost time for our meal in the nurse's sitting room. You'll be glad of the break, I'm sure, Delia. I know I was when I first started here. I even dreamed I was scouring out bed pans in my sleep!'

'See, I told you we all go through it,' Evie said, hoping that Delia would manage to keep going. This job was the worst one the VADs did, so from here, the only way was up for their newest recruit.

CHAPTER 5

'We're going to create a pattern from a garment you love but which has become worn out from so much wear. Have you all brought something to work from?' Marianne cast her gaze over the women sitting around the large table set out at one end of Great Plumstead village hall, many of whom were members of The Mother's Day Club which had been set up for evacuee mothers and their children. She was pleased to see nods of agreement, several women pointing to some folded clothing on the table in front of them.

'This is a favourite dress of mine and I've worn it so much the material's become that thin in places it's almost see-through.' Gloria held up a bright, fuchsia-pink dress. 'It's a wonder it ain't ripped open and shown off me underclothes and 'ad the village constable after me tellin' me to cover meself up! If I can make another one in the same style, then I'll be grinning like the Cheshire Cat.' She curled her pillar-box-red lips into a wide, beaming smile, before breaking into a throaty chuckle.

Laughing along with the other women, Marianne thought

how much she loved East Ender Gloria's sunny, humorous and down-to-earth attitude. 'I'm sure you'll be able to and you can keep the pattern to create more dresses like it in the future, too.'

Marianne picked up the old blouse of Hettie's that she'd brought along to demonstrate with, having promised to make her friend a new one from the pattern she created.

'I'm going to use this blouse to show you what to do. The first thing, before you do anything else, is to have a close look at your garment. You're probably so used to it that you haven't noticed how it's been constructed. Or even how many pieces it is made from? It's important to know this because you're going to be taking it apart and must understand how to put the parts together to make a new garment. With this blouse,' Marianne held it up for the women to see, 'it has two front pieces, and each of those comprises two parts…' She pointed out the parts and went on to indicate all the other individual components that made up the blouse. 'You need to think of it in the same way a house is constructed. Look at which bits join with which, where and how. Then when your garment is taken apart and you've made your pattern from it, you won't get in a muddle when you're ready to sew the pieces of fabric together. Taking time at the start will pay off. Now, before we go any further, take a few minutes to study your garment carefully. Make a drawing of it if that helps.' She pointed to some sheets of paper and pencils on the table.

While the women busied themselves investigating how their garments were made, Marianne glanced around at the other groups who were busy as part of this afternoon's Make and Mend party. Prue, Thea's sister and instigator of the party and so much else in the village, was working with a group who were making some children's coats from old blankets.

Hettie was helping some women knitting socks and gloves. Everyone was busy.

Since they'd started having these parties back in June, they'd proven very popular. The women, both local and evacuees, were becoming more proficient at making the most out of the limited resources they had to clothe themselves and their families. Marianne loved sharing her dressmaking skills with them and it was rewarding to see even the most inexperienced sewer start to blossom and grow more confident.

'I ain't ever looked at this properly before.' Annie, another of the evacuees, held up the old skirt she'd brought to show Marianne. 'I never would 'ave thought it 'ad so many pieces in it!'

'When we stop to study something, it's surprising what we notice,' Marianne said. 'So now you've all had a good look, we'll move on.'

She turned Hettie's old blouse inside out and held it up, so the women could see the seams. 'The next job is to unpick the seams to separate the individual pieces. This needs to be done carefully so you don't damage the fabric, remember it's worn thin in places.' She took her unpicking tool out of her sewing box and removed the lid covering the sharp end. 'I'm going to start with the side seams.' She put the blouse on the table and, using the unpicker, carefully cut through a few stitches and then used her fingers to ease the pieces away from each other and then repeated the process. Marianne held up the blouse again. 'I've made a start, but it's going to take a while to do it carefully. Make a start on your garments and remember take your time with your unpicking. If you're unsure of anything, just ask before you cut any stitches!'

As the women got to work, Marianne made her way

around the table, looking over their shoulders at how they were getting on.

'It's fiddly!' Nancy, who lived with Prue, said as she unpicked one of her daughters' old dresses. 'I suppose the smaller the garment, the fiddlier it is.'

'Yes, the ratio of seams to fabric is higher than on adult clothes. You're doing well,' Marianne reassured her. 'Just keep taking your time.'

Nancy looked up and nodded. 'Thanks.'

Marianne was pleased to see that everyone was focused on their work and concentrating hard.

By the time Prue came into the hall wheeling the trolley loaded with the urn and cups for their tea break, most of the women had managed to unpick their garment and were ready to move onto the next stage.

'After our tea break, we'll start making the paper patterns from the pieces of fabric you've unpicked,' Marianne said. 'I've brought some spare newspaper if anyone hasn't got any paper with them.'

'I've got some spare, too,' Gloria added.

'Thank you.' Marianne gave Gloria a smile. 'The seamstress I worked for in London would be horrified at us using *newspaper* for making patterns but needs must, as they say.'

'We ain't fussy,' Nancy declared. 'It's about making do and mending. Using what we've got.'

'Exactly,' Marianne agreed. 'Let's have a well-earned break.'

Taking her cup of tea, Marianne went over to the far end of the hall to check on Emily. Her daughter was in the safety of the children's area, along with other small children, who were being looked after by a couple of the mothers. Emily was happily playing with a tea set along with Dora, Gloria's daughter.

'Ain't they sweet!' Gloria said in a hushed voice, coming to stand beside Marianne. 'I love watching how they play make-believe with the tea set.'

Marianne laughed. 'They copy what they see, I suppose.'

'Shall we take the weight off our feet for a bit?' Gloria asked.

'Yes, that would be good,' Marianne agreed.

They made their way over to some chairs set out at the side of the hall not far from the children's area and sat down.

'It's tiring work concentrating on unpicking seams! I daren't talk in case I cut through the wrong bit. Being quiet ain't like me as you know!' Gloria gave a low throaty laugh.

Marianne raised an eyebrow. 'I thought you were unusually quiet!'

'It's a rare occurrence, to be sure.' Gloria shifted in her seat so that she was facing Marianne. 'Are you all right, ducks? Only you look tired if you don't mind me saying so. Is the baby keeping you awake at night?'

Marianne lowered the cup she'd just taken a sip from. 'I am tired, and no, I don't mind you asking.' She paused for a moment before going on. 'I couldn't settle to sleep for hours last night. It was a full moon, a bomber's moon. I was worrying about Alex up there…' Her voice tailed off.

Gloria grabbed hold of Marianne's free hand and gave it a squeeze. 'I understand, ducks. I've been there myself many a time. Not because of a full moon in my case, 'cause my Charlie ain't an airman, but I worry about 'im every day out there crossing the Atlantic being hunted down by enemy submarines.' She gave a heartfelt sigh. 'I know there ain't a single thing I can do to 'elp 'im apart from praying he will come through this, but it don't stop me worrying about 'im.'

'It's awful, isn't it?' Marianne's eyes filled with tears and she blinked them away. 'Feeling so helpless?'

Gloria nodded, making her bottle-blonde pompadour-styled hair bob on top of her head. 'It is. And we've just got to accept it because it's out of our control. But I'm always 'ere to talk to anytime you want to. I understand what it's like.'

'Thank you, I appreciate that.' Marianne gave her a grateful smile.

The rattle of the trolley coming towards them caught Marianne's attention.

'More tea, ladies?' Prue asked.

Marianne drank the last of her tea. 'Yes, please, I'd love another cup.'

'Any news from your lad in North Africa, Prue?' Gloria asked as Prue refilled their cups from the urn.

'I had a letter from Edwin yesterday. He's fine, doing well. He likes what he's doing and being in a different place, all except for the flies and sand that gets everywhere.' Prue handed Marianne her cup.

'Thank you. It must feel like a stark contrast from here, that's for sure,' Marianne said. 'If it hadn't been for the war, he'd probably never have got to travel there.'

'And I'd never 'ave come 'ere neither,' Gloria said. 'Much as I don't like the war, I do like being 'ere and 'aving made so many friends at The Mother's Day Club.'

'Same with me,' Marianne agreed. 'It's one of the good things that's come out of the war.'

'They say every cloud has a silver lining,' Prue added. 'Without clothes rationing, we probably wouldn't be having this Make and Mend party. You wouldn't be helping so many women to improve their sewing skills.'

'I really enjoy it,' Marianne said. 'And everyone's keen and they're good learners.'

Gloria nodded, puffing her ample bosom out. 'Indeed, we are. I'm looking forward to being able to make some more copies of my favourite outfits. My landlady Sylvia's got some old curtains she's said I can have, so I'll be making them into a dress. And I've got my eye on a tablecloth she ain't never used, too.'

'There'll be no stopping you, Gloria,' Prue said.

Marianne laughed, her spirits rising. She may have started the early hours of the day awake and worrying, but coming here, being amongst these women who'd become friends, while sharing her love of sewing, had given her a much-needed boost. 'Come on Gloria, we'd better drink up and get back to work so you can make your pattern!'

CHAPTER 6

'Smell that air!' Violet paused to breath in deeply. 'The scent of autumn.' She turned to face Thea. 'It's so lovely to be out of London again.'

Thea gave her friend a warm smile, delighted how much joy a simple walk in the nearby woods was bringing Violet. Since her arrival yesterday, she had already begun to relax.

'That's not a smell you get in London,' Thea said. 'There, it's more exhaust fumes and chimney smoke, something I certainly don't miss. I often wonder how I managed to live there for so long.' She shook her head. 'Mind you, I escaped back here as often as I could for a dose of the space and greenery of the countryside. That probably helped me cope.'

'It's such a contrast,' Violet said as they fell into step again, walking beneath the tall trees, a mixture of beech, oak, sweet chestnut and smaller hazel. 'I suppose it depends on where you grow up as to how you feel about the city or the countryside. I know for sure that some of my crew would struggle being out here. They are city dwellers through and through. When I sent Sparky on a week's stay to a Red Cross

Country Hospitality Scheme house, he couldn't wait to get back to London! He was supposed to be resting after working through the Blitz, but he told me he just couldn't settle. There was too much green space around him, and it was too quiet for him. He ended up coming home early and took some rest at home in the East End, surrounded by bomb sites and row after row of buildings.'

'A similar thing happened with some of the evacuee mothers we've had in the village,' Thea said, her feet crunching over fallen leaves. 'They couldn't stand it here and had to return to the city, even though there was a risk of bombing.'

'Is that what happened with George and Betty's mother?' Violet asked, glancing at Thea.

'No, I think Jess went back to keep an eye on her husband! At least she had the sense to leave her children here where they're safe from the bombing.'

'They both seem very settled with you at Rookery House,' Violet said. 'And from the look of it, you're very happy looking after them.'

Thea nodded. 'I am. I know George and Betty aren't my children, but it's giving me a taste of what it would be like to be a mother, something I never thought I'd have. Not after losing Tom.'

Violet tucked her hand through Thea's arm. 'The Great War has a lot to answer for.' She let out a sigh. 'It changed the futures of so many people. Robbing us of the chance to be wives and mothers.'

Thea patted her friend's hand, and they fell silent for a few moments as they walked along arm in arm. Thea's thoughts went back to her fiancé Tom, who she'd lost on the battlefields of France but whom she would never forget or stop loving. She was sure Violet's thoughts were similar thinking of her fiancé, William, who'd succumbed to shell shock after two years at the front, had been court-martialled for desertion and shot by his own side. It had been a terrible, terrible time and should never have been allowed to happen to any soldier. It was cruel and wrong. But like so much of what had happened in the Great War, with the loss of so many lives, the destiny of individuals was out of their own control ruled by leaders who had no compassion or even experience of the realities of what the soldiers in the trenches went through.

Thea brought her attention back to the here and now, the surrounding trees, the crunch of their feet on the fallen leaves, the sounds of birds. It didn't do to dwell too deeply on the past and things that could not even be changed then, because with the passage of time, they certainly couldn't be now.

They'd almost reached the edge of the wood from where, in the distance, they could see machinery in action over on what was the developing aerodrome being built between the villages of Great Plumstead and Geswick.

'Is that the new aerodrome?' Violet asked as they stopped at the edge of the tree line and peered across.

'They've started building the second runway now, so Reuben tells me. My brother's taken a great interest in what's going on. There's been truck after truck carrying cement for it from Wykeham station. By the time they've finished, there will be a lot of ground that used to be farmland concreted over,' Thea explained.

'How do you feel about having an aerodrome on your doorstep?' Violet asked, glancing at Thea.

'I suppose they've got to go somewhere,' Thea replied. 'Though it's caused a lot of disruption around the area, taking over land and homes to start with, and now the building. Once it's operational we'll be affected by the noise and more servicemen around. But right from the start of this war, things have been changing around here and they'll keep on changing until it's over. We just must accept it and get on with things.'

'You've always been very stoical,' Violet said.

Thea shrugged a shoulder. 'I am about *some* things, but I'm not a pushover either. If something needs sorting out, I'll see to it.'

Violet raised an eyebrow. 'Like when your Jewish German refugee was arrested and sent to the camp on the Isle of Man? It was awful and completely unjustified, and you didn't rest until she was freed. How is Anna?'

'She's very well, enjoying teaching at the school in Wiltshire. She came back in August for a visit, and it was lovely to see her,' Thea said. 'She'll be back for the Christmas holidays too.'

'That's good to hear. Now, didn't you say something about collecting some food for your pigs?' Violet asked. 'Since we're in the woods, we might as well get some. We can at least fill up our coat pockets. I always used to love collecting chestnuts when I was a child. There's something very satisfying about gathering food from the wild.'

'All right, let's do that,' Thea agreed. 'It's a little early for the chestnuts to be ready, but the acorns are starting to fall, and the pigs will enjoy how ever many we can take back for them.'

CHAPTER 7

Evie finished the last mouthful of the delicious jam roly-poly and custard and placed her spoon in her empty bowl. Hettie had left it, along with her first course of shepherd's pie, in the warming oven of the range as everyone else at Rookery House had already eaten their evening meal before Evie arrived home after her long shift at work. Tonight, it was just Evie in the kitchen, as Hettie had gone out with Flo to the Great Plumstead Village Singing Group. Evie was glad of some quiet time on her own after the busy day she'd had.

Sitting back in her chair, her thoughts turned to Delia, the new VAD, whose arrival at the hospital yesterday had reminded Evie of her own difficult start there. She smiled to herself, thinking that she'd come a long way since then and was happy working there and hoped that, in time, Delia would be too.

The door from the hallway opened and Thea came in.

'Hello, have you had a good day?'

Evie nodded. 'Yes, it's been busy as usual.'

'I'm going to make some cocoa for Violet and myself. Would you like some?' Thea asked.

'Oh yes, please. I'll get the cups ready.' Evie stood up.

'Thanks. Have you seen there's a letter for you on the dresser? It came in the afternoon post,' Thea said, before heading into the pantry.

Evie's immediate thought was that it might be from Ned Blythe, but as she walked over to the dresser, she spotted the envelope propped up against a plate and knew it wasn't. It was bigger than the ones Ned used and looked official, with her name and address typed on the front. It sent a trickle of unease creeping down her spine. Picking it up, Evie turned the letter over and saw no clue who it was from, but instinct told her this was something she should read when she was alone. She slipped it into the pocket of her dress to open later in the privacy of her bedroom.

'Did you find it?' Thea asked, returning from the pantry with a jug of milk and the tin of cocoa.

'Yes, I'll read it later.' Evie put three mugs down on the table. 'Is Marianne having some cocoa too?'

'No, she's gone up to bed early. She gets tired quicker these days,' Thea explained, pouring milk into a saucepan and then setting it on the range to warm up.

'It's no wonder Marianne's tired out. She's got an energetic small child to look after as well as being an expectant mother,' Evie said.

They chatted for a while longer, Evie asking Thea about her day, until the cocoa was ready.

'Violet and I are listening to the wireless. Would you like to join us?' Thea asked.

'I won't, thanks. I'm tired so I think I'll take my drink up to my bedroom and read for a while.'

Thea gave her an understanding smile. 'Of course. Enjoy your book.'

Upstairs, sitting on her bed, a lit candle throwing out a soft-yellow glow, Evie took the envelope out of her pocket, noticing the thick creamy paper looked expensive. Who it was from or what it was about she didn't know. There was only one way to find out and that was by opening it.

Evie took a deep breath, ripped the envelope, took out the single sheet of paper and opened it. Her eyes were drawn to the printed header at the top of the letter: *Willoughby, Chase and Haynes Solicitors*. Their address was in London. Evie's stomach knotted. She knew of them – they were the solicitors that her husband had used. What did they want with her?

Chewing on her bottom lip, Evie's eyes skimmed downwards, quickly reading through the letter.

Dear Mrs Hamilton-Jones,

I am writing to you as the solicitor of your late husband, Captain Douglas Hamilton-Jones.
It has taken me some time to find your whereabouts as I had been informed that you'd been killed in the Blitz. However, it has recently come to my attention, via an acquaintance of my wife who knows your mother, that I had been badly misinformed. I was glad to hear that you are, in fact, alive and well and now living in Norfolk. I assume your reported demise was because of a mistaken identification in the chaos after an air raid.
As Captain Hamilton-Jones' wife, you are a beneficiary of

his will. I would appreciate it if you could telephone me at
my office at your earliest convenience to arrange a meeting.
I look forward to hearing from you.

Yours sincerely

Mr A. D. Willoughby

Evie dropped the letter as if it had burnt her and stood up, her heart pounding and her body shaking. She wanted nothing from Douglas. She may have been his wife, but he'd never cared for her or treated her well. The thought of taking anything from him, even now he was dead and could no longer harm her, made her feel utterly sick. Evie had escaped and was living a free, happy life. After years of being controlled, physically hurt and belittled by him, her new life was filled with joy and good, kind-hearted people who were her dear friends. She wanted to forget all about Douglas.

Blinking away tears, Evie hurried over to her bookcase and ran a finger along the spines. She needed to read. To lose herself in a favourite book, as she'd often done back in the dark days of her marriage. Books had been her sanctuary, her escape. Douglas touching her life again, no matter how remotely, had brought out her instinct to seek refuge within the pages of a book. She selected one of her favourites, *Pride and Prejudice*, went over to her bed and lay down on top of the covers, pulling a blanket over her. Her head resting on the soft, feather pillow, she opened the book and began to read.

Evie was engrossed in the scene where Elizabeth Bennet arrives at Netherfield to care for her poorly sister, when the bedroom door opened, and Flo came in having returned from her evening with the village singing group.

Evie glanced at the alarm clock on the nightstand between the two beds and saw that nearly an hour had passed since she'd started reading.

'Thea said you'd come up to read. Are you all right?'

Evie pulled herself up into a sitting position and leaned back against the black iron bedstead.

'Yes…' Her voice tailed off as the emotions of earlier rushed back and her eyes filled with tears. 'Actually, no I'm not.'

Flo hurried over and sat down on the edge of Evie's bed, a concerned look on her face. 'What's wrong?'

Evie swallowed hard and gestured towards the sheet of paper on the floor between their beds where it still lay after she'd dropped it.

'Have you had bad news? I saw there was a letter for you on the dresser earlier.'

'Read it,' Evie said, relieved to have someone to share the news with. She'd revealed the truth to Flo about her marriage to Douglas and her escape from London during one of their many chats a few months ago. Flo was one of the few people here at Rookery House who knew Evie's full story.

She watched as Flo picked up the letter and read it through before placing it on the nightstand between their beds.

'That must have been a shock. What do you think he's left you?'

'Whatever it is I don't want *anything* from him,' Evie snapped. 'I'm sorry.' She shook her head. 'This letter has stirred up so many painful memories for me. I thought I'd escaped from Douglas and now that he's dead he could never affect me again but…' She lifted her hands. 'Here I am feeling so…' She paused to search for the right words to explain the tumultuous emotions inside her that the letter had stirred up. 'It's dragged me back to how I felt before I escaped. Reminded me of the fear I lived in, the control. Douglas ruled my life then, I don't want anything from him tainting my new life. Whatever he's left me, I do *not* want it!'

Flo nodded, her eyes full of sympathy. 'I understand. But perhaps it might be worth finding out before you refuse anything, don't you think? You can always turn it down. He may have left something to say sorry for what he did to you.'

Evie frowned. 'I doubt that very much. Douglas never saw the way he behaved and treated people as wrong.'

Flo patted Evie's arm. 'You've had a shock. Take your time to consider it and then decide. It's never a good idea to make snap decisions, especially where emotions are involved.'

Evie couldn't help smiling at her friend's sage words. 'I suppose you're right. I'll think about it, but I honestly don't expect I will change my mind. I'll probably just ignore the letter and pretend I never got it.'

'Until the next one arrives. Mr Willoughby might not give up so easily till he gets a reply,' Flo warned.

Evie pursed her lips. 'We shall see. In the meantime, I'm going to get ready for bed and then return to my sanctuary of *Pride and Prejudice.*' Leaving her book on the bedcovers, she stood up. 'Please don't tell anyone what the letter was about will you?'

'Of course not. I promise not to breathe a word about it,' Flo said in an earnest voice.

Evie nodded and gave her friend a grateful smile. 'Thank you.'

As she headed out onto the landing and made her way down the stairs to the bathroom, Evie considered what Flo had said. Evie would think about it but after everything she'd gone through, she doubted her opinion would alter.

CHAPTER 8

The sunshine of the past few days had gone, replaced by heavy grey skies with the promise of rain and a sharp north wind. Buffeted by gusts as she bicycled along the road heading to the hospital, Evie thought the weather matched the way she felt this morning – dull with tiredness and full of turmoil. It was all because of the news the letter had brought her.

Despite her talk with Flo before bed last night, Evie's mind had refused to quieten and allow her to drift into sleep when she'd finally blown out the candle after reading more chapters of *Pride and Prejudice*. Instead, it had gone round and round, thinking about what she should do. When she had finally drifted off in the early hours of this morning, Evie's dreams had turned into a nightmare, taking her back to the days of living in London with Douglas. As he'd lunged at her and raised his hand to strike, she'd woken with a start, her heart pounding in her chest and her body shaking. After that, she had lain awake staring up into the darkness waiting for the alarm to go off.

Turning off the road between the two gatehouses and onto

the long drive to the Hall, Evie was grateful to be heading to work. She needed to keep herself busy in the hope it would distract her, allow the weight that now hung over her like the leaden clouds above to fade into the background for a while. There was nothing she could do to deal with the letter today while she was on her shift. She must focus on her work, Evie told herself as a powerful gust made the beech trees lining the drive roar and their branches sway, sending their golden leaves skittering down to the ground. She put her head down against the wind and pedalled harder.

Sorting through the laundry delivery was a job that Evie usually enjoyed. There was something restful about the clean smelling piles of freshly washed and ironed white sheets and pillowcases. Their smoothness and neatness were a welcome contrast from the busyness of other jobs she did. It was always quiet here, in what had been the Butler's pantry, where the large, glass-fronted cupboards were perfect for storing clean bed linen.

Matron had tasked Evie with the job of checking that what had been delivered tallied with the chit that came with the laundry, as well as the record of the number of sheets and pillowcases that had been sent out to be washed. She'd also been told to do an inventory of the bed linen in the cupboards. It was one of the weekly tasks Matron gave out, where staff had to check there was enough equipment and supplies to keep the hospital running smoothly.

The problem was that although Evie had counted through the large pile of sheets returned from the laundry three times; she had come up with a different amount each time. How difficult could it be to count sheets? she chided herself. She dropped the clipboard with the laundry chit on it down onto the table and counted once more. What was the matter with her? She usually had no difficulty doing this job and enjoyed putting things in order. But today… Evie knew what was wrong – she wasn't concentrating properly, and it was because of the letter and the horror of her past life with Douglas rearing its ugly, terrifying head again. He might be dead, buried in a grave in a foreign land, so she'd heard, but he still had the power to bring turmoil and upset to her.

Evie shook her head, trying to rid herself of thinking about him, to stop it affecting her work. She closed her eyes and let out a heavy sigh. Tomorrow was her day off and would give her a chance to telephone the solicitor if that's what she decided to do. In the meantime, she needed to *concentrate*, she told herself, firmly. Just *focus* on the sheets, nothing more.

'I take it you've finished your job if you've time to stand there with your eyes closed, Nurse Jones,' a soft Scottish voice said.

Evie's eyes snapped open. Standing in the doorway was the portly figure of Matron Reed, her eyes fixed on Evie's face.

'Although from the state of things in here,' the older woman advanced into the room, 'you clearly haven't! All that bed linen needs to be put away in the cupboards.'

'I… I…' Evie stammered, her cheeks growing hot.

Matron picked up the clipboard, her shrewd brown eyes scanning over the chit before raising them to stare at Evie. 'How many sheets have they delivered from the laundry this morning? Is it fifty-six, fifty-nine or sixty?' Her voice was sharp as she jabbed her finger at the figures on the chit where Evie had pencilled them in. 'You seem to have lost the ability to count accurately, Nurse Jones.' She checked the list which documented what had been sent to the laundry earlier in the week. 'We sent sixty sheets there, and I expected the same number back, so either they didn't return them all or you aren't doing your job properly. Which is it?'

Tears prickled behind Evie's eyes. She curled her hands into tight fists behind her back. She would not show Matron how she felt. Evie had learned long ago in the early days of her marriage to hide her emotions.

'I think I've made a mistake,' Evie said, forcing her voice to sound normal.

'Not *a* mistake, but *two* if you came up with incorrect figures twice!' Matron snapped. 'This is a straightforward, simple job, Nurse Jones. One you are quite capable of, and I expect it to be done with care and accuracy. If you can't do it properly, then perhaps you should be placed on basic duties in the sluice again.' Matron raised an eyebrow, tapping her foot on the stone floor. 'Do I need to send for another nurse to do the job?'

'No, Matron. I'm sorry I made a mistake. It won't happen again,' Evie said, her cheeks feeling as if they were on fire.

'I hope not.' Matron glanced around at the cupboards full of sheets and pillowcases. 'You still need to do the inventory on the rest of the bed linen. I will return in…' she glanced at the watch pinned to the front of her dress, 'forty-five minutes and will double check you have done an accurate count, and if there's so much as one missed item, you will be back in the sluice for the rest of week.'

'Yes, Matron.' Evie knew that the older woman would keep to her word. She expected her staff to do their jobs correctly.

'I will return at half past two, so you'd best get on with it.' Matron turned on her polished black shoes and marched out.

Evie slumped against the table, her head hanging as tears blurred her vision, causing the piles of white folded bed linen before her to swim and distort. She was cross with herself for making a mess of such a straightforward task. It wasn't like her. She had to pull herself together because if she was incapable of doing a simple task such as this correctly, then she feared making a more serious mistake with a patient. With that in mind, Matron was justified in her threat to put Evie back to working in the sluice alongside Delia. Getting into Matron's bad books was the last thing she needed on top of worrying what to do about being a beneficiary of Douglas's will. Right now, doing her job properly was what mattered.

She stood up straight, took a deep breath and began to carefully count through the pile of neatly ironed sheets once more.

CHAPTER 9

Marianne leaned back into the soft brown leather seat, watching the rain trickle down the outside of the car window. With a warm red tartan blanket tucked over her legs, she was grateful that Lady Campbell-Gryce had insisted that she sent her chauffeur to pick Marianne up. Being driven in an expensive car along the beech tree lined driveway towards Great Plumstead Hall was a sharp contrast to Marianne's usual mode of transport – her feet – and with the weather so foul today, she appreciated the luxury.

This morning her Ladyship had telephoned Rookery House, asking if Marianne would come and see her. She wanted Marianne to design and make a new dress for her. It wouldn't be the first time that Lady Campbell-Gryce had used Marianne's designing and dressmaking services, as she'd been a regular customer since Marianne had first started her business after being evacuated to the village in the autumn of 1939. After Marianne had married Alex, she'd had a less urgent need to earn money than before when she was on her own, but she'd still carried on doing some work, now more for her love of it than needing to provide an income. Although with a small child to care for, Marianne had much less time to devote to it than she'd had in the past.

'It's a good job her Ladyship sent the car for you, otherwise you'd have been drenched by the time you reached the Hall,' the chauffeur said, his eyes glancing at her in the rear-view mirror.

'She was most insistent, and with this rain, I wasn't going to turn the offer down,' Marianne replied. 'And it's a treat to have a ride in a car like this!'

'It's not used very much these days compared to how things were before the war,' the chauffeur told her. 'I've been drafted in to assist in the hospital when I'm not needed to drive, and that makes me feel more like I'm helping with the war effort. I couldn't serve in the forces because I had rheumatic fever as a child and it left its mark on the heart.'

'I'm sure your help is much appreciated in the hospital,' Marianne said.

Coming to a halt in front of the Hall, the chauffeur turned off the engine and got out, putting up an umbrella before opening the back door for Marianne to step out.

'I'll take you round to the west wing where Lord and Lady Campbell-Gryce now live,' the chauffeur explained as he led Marianne around the side of the house rather than going in the front door which led into the hospital.

Their arrival was clearly expected, as the chauffeur had barely raised his hand to knock on the door of the west wing when it was opened from the inside by a familiar face.

'Good morning, Marianne,' Hettie's sister Ada said, looking very smart in a navy-blue dress. 'Her Ladyship is expecting you.' She stepped aside and gestured for Marianne to enter.

'Hello, Ada.' Turning to the chauffeur, Marianne gave him a grateful smile. 'Thank you for bringing me.'

'You're welcome. I'll take you home again when you're ready.' He touched the brow of his peaked cap.

'Can I take your coat for you?' Ada asked, closing the front door behind them.

Marianne took her coat off and handed it to Ada who hung it up on a coat stand in the corner of the hall. 'If you'd like to follow me.' She led the way across a hallway which was, Marianne noticed, much smaller than the one in the main part of the house. 'Her Ladyship is in her sitting room.'

Stopping outside the door, Ada knocked on it and, hearing a voice call 'Come in' from inside, opened it and they both stepped in. 'Mrs Fordham is here to see you, your Ladyship,' Ada announced.

'Thank you, Mrs Kilburn. Could you have some tea brought through to us, please?' Lady Campbell-Gryce said in her plummy voice.

'Certainly, your Ladyship,' Ada said before leaving the room, quietly closing the door behind her.

Lady Campbell-Gryce greeted Marianne with a welcoming smile. 'Thank you so much for coming here this afternoon. Do take a seat.' She indicated an armchair opposite where she was sitting next to the fireplace where a fire burned brightly, warming the room.

Marianne sat down opposite the older woman and took out a notebook and a pencil from her handbag, before placing it on the floor by her feet.

'I hope you're still enjoying teaching the women of the village how to make more of their own clothes at the Make and Mend parties,' Lady Campbell-Gryce said.

'I am very much. All the women are enthusiastic and keen to learn. It's a pleasure to teach them.'

'We are lucky to have you living here in Great Plumstead and able to share your considerable dressmaking skills.' The older woman gave Marianne a warm smile. 'In keeping with clothes rationing and the need to make the most of the resources we have, I would like you to design and make a dress for me using fabric from any of these.' She waved her hand towards two piles of folded material on the table by the window, which Marianne had noticed when she'd come in. 'They are old curtains, tablecloths and bed linen. I had Mrs Kilburn hunt them out for me from where they'd been packed away sometime in the past. All perfectly good serviceable cloth, I believe. I will rely on your expertise to judge what you think is best to use.'

'May I have a look?' Marianne asked.

'Of course.' Lady Campbell-Gryce stood up and made her way over to the piles of fabric.

Marianne followed, her eyes drawn to the different colours and textures. She reached out and ran her fingers over the wine-red velvet on top of one pile.

'Those are some curtains, I believe. They used to hang in a bedroom in the main part of the house.' Lady Campbell-Gryce took a curtain from the pile and shook it out, holding her arms up high, but even then the fabric pooled on the carpet.

'There's a lot of material there.' Marianne stroked her hand over the soft, sumptuous fabric. 'Plenty to make a dress with.'

'And there are two of them as well,' Lady Campbell-Gryce pointed out. 'Let's have a look at the rest of what we've got.' She draped the curtain over the back of a chair by the table and took another item from the pile, this time a much thinner, flower printed fabric, and held it up. 'This is a tablecloth.'

Marianne felt the fabric between her fingers and thumb. 'This is lighter weight than the velvet, better suited to a summer garment. It's a lovely pattern.'

By the time Ada returned with a loaded tea tray, Marianne and Lady Campbell-Gryce had had a good look through the piles of fabric.

'Thank you, Mrs Kilburn,' her Ladyship said as Ada put the tea things down on the little table beside the armchairs near the fire.

'Do you need me to find any more old curtains or anything?' Ada asked, her eyes taking in the chair that was draped in a colourful assortment of material.

'I think we've got something suitable to use from this lot, haven't we?' Lady Campbell-Gryce directed her question at Marianne.

'Most definitely,' Marianne agreed. 'There's enough material there to make many garments.'

Lady Campbell-Gryce nodded. 'So no, but thank you Mrs Kilburn. You did an excellent job searching these out for me.'

'Thank you.' Ada looked pleased.

'I'll ring the bell when we've finished,' her Ladyship said, dismissing Ada, who gave a nod of her head and left the room. 'Now, Marianne, let's have some tea and some of Mrs Shepherd's delicious scones and we can talk about what you're going to make for me.'

Settled back in the armchairs, with her cup of tea and a warm scone topped with butter and jam, Marianne considered which was the best material to use. 'I think the wine-red velvet would work well if you're looking for a winter dress and it would work well for Christmas too. It's a warm fabric, and the colour is lovely. It will suit you well. When would you want it ready by?'

Lady Campbell-Gryce put the teacup she'd just taken a sip from back on its saucer. 'Whenever you can get it done by. I know you have little Emily to care for and a new baby on the way.' Her eyes drifted down briefly to Marianne's rounded belly. 'I appreciate you have much less time and energy these days to devote to designing and dressmaking. I'm prepared to wait because I value your excellent work.'

Marianne gave the older woman a grateful smile. 'Thank you. I appreciate your understanding of my situation. I'm doing far less work than I used to, but still want to carry on when possible because I love it so much. I'd enjoy making another dress for you and will get it done for you as soon as I can, but I can't give you a specific date.'

Lady Campbell-Gryce nodded. 'That's absolutely fine. Now I have a few ideas for the design, but please do tell me if you think they won't be right for me. I trust your judgement.'

Marianne opened her notebook ready to listen to her Ladyship's ideas. They spent a very pleasant half hour talking through design features from sleeve length to shape of neckline and hem length, each decision they made helping her draft a design, sketching out potential ideas in her book.

'What do you think of this?' Marianne showed the latest sketch to Lady Campbell-Gryce.

The older woman studied the design for a few moments and then gave Marianne a beaming smile. 'It's perfect. I can just see it in the velvet. It's going to look beautiful.'

'I think so too,' Marianne agreed.

'Excellent. I'll have Mrs Kilburn parcel the velvet curtains up so that you can take them home with you.' Lady Campbell-Gryce rang the bell that stood on the little table beside her chair. 'I'm delighted to be working with you on a dress once more. It's always such fun.'

'Thank you, it will be fun for me, too.' Marianne said.

CHAPTER 10

Evie perched on the bottom step of Rookery House's stairs, staring at the black Bakelite telephone standing on a small table. She'd been here for the past five minutes, willing herself to get on with it, but still not sure if she was doing the right thing, or not. You're scared, Evie told herself, which wasn't surprising after what Douglas had put her through. But he was gone now and she was free. He couldn't hurt her again.

All she had to do was make the telephone call and listen to what Mr Willoughby said. If she didn't want to accept the bequest then she didn't have to. What was important was that she must do something to put this behind her as it had affected her badly, even to the point of making her careless at work. Evie had been fortunate yesterday that when Matron Reed had returned to check on her inventory of the bed linen, Evie's counting had been accurate, and she'd avoided a demotion to working in the sluice. She knew Matron would be keeping a close eye on her in case she slipped up again, so she didn't have a choice but to sort this out, did she? The sooner she got on with it, the sooner it would be done with.

Now was the perfect time. The house was quiet as Hettie and Marianne had gone to The Mother's Day Club, while Thea, Flo, Thea's niece Alice and Violet were somewhere outside and the children at school. No one was around to overhear what she was saying. Evie had asked Thea if it was alright for her to make a telephone call to London but hadn't told her why. Thea had been fine about it and respecting Evie's privacy hadn't asked who it would be to.

Evie stood up, squared her shoulders, took the solicitor's letter from her pocket, and picked up the receiver. She waited for the operator's voice to come down the line, asking which number she required, then read out the London number from the top of the letter.

As Evie listened to the ringing tone, she was aware of her heart beating harder in her chest.

'Good morning, Willoughby, Chase and Haynes, Solicitors, how may I help you?' a crisply efficient woman's voice asked.

'I'd like to speak to Mr Willoughby, please. My name is Genevieve Hamilton-Jones and Mr Willoughby has asked me to telephone him,' Evie explained.

'One moment please,' the woman said.

Evie waited, focusing on her breathing, keeping it slow and steady. Keep calm, she told herself, this would be over in a matter of minutes.

'Good morning, Mrs Hamilton-Jones, Mr Willoughby here,' a man's deep voice broke into her thoughts. 'Thank you for telephoning me. What date would you like to come in and see me so we can discuss the bequest your late husband has left you?'

Panic flared in Evie. The last thing she wanted was to go down to London to his office, even if she could have the time off from the hospital.

'I'm afraid that's impossible. I'm a nurse at a hospital for wounded servicemen and can't take any leave to come to London as we're extremely busy. Can't you tell me now?'

'It's highly irregular…' he began.

'There's a war on and that makes many things highly irregular,' Evie cut in. 'We all have to make allowances these days.'

'Very well. Your late husband, Captain Douglas Hamilton-Jones, has left you the sum of…' Evie could hear the rustling of papers for several moments, imagining the solicitor rummaging about on his desk to find the correct document. 'Five thousand pounds. That may come as a shock to you, as you'll be aware that Captain Hamilton-Jones' estate was worth more than that, but he bequeathed the rest to his parents. They were the majority beneficiaries of his estate.'

Evie shook her head. Even in death, Douglas had shown her what he thought of her. He hadn't left her *without* a legacy, as that would have looked badly on him. Douglas had been all about show and how others perceived him, while behind closed doors, it was quite the opposite and Evie had been the victim of his true nature. Considering his wealth, what he'd bequeathed to her was just enough to meet his duty as a husband, but no more.

'Mrs Hamilton-Jones?' Mr Willoughby's voice had a note of concern. 'Are you all right?'

'Yes, I'm fine,' she reassured him.

'As his wife, you may have expected to be the sole or at least the majority beneficiary of your late husband's will?' he probed.

'To be honest, Mr Willoughby, I hadn't thought about it,' Evie said truthfully, because she wanted nothing from Douglas.

'Captain Hamilton-Jones made this will shortly before he was posted overseas. He told me about his reasoning for his lower bequest for you. He said that if he should be killed while serving in the army, then you would still be a young woman and therefore likely to remarry in due course and your new husband could provide for you. That's why he bequeathed the bulk of his estate to his parents,' he explained. 'It keeps most of his money in his family.'

'It was his to do with as he chose,' Evie said. She didn't care who Douglas had left his money to. 'I'm not planning on remarrying. In fact, I don't…'

'You must excuse me, I'm late for my next appointment,' Mr Willoughby cut in. 'I will arrange for a cheque to be sent to you. If there's anything else I can help you with, get in touch. I bid you a good day.'

Evie opened her mouth to speak, but he had already disconnected the call. She returned the telephone receiver to its cradle and let out a heavy sigh, relieved that it was over. Douglas might have left her some money, but it did not mean she had to accept it and cash the cheque from the solicitor!

Sitting down on the stairs again, Evie leaned her elbows on her knees and put her head in her hands. What was the best thing to do? Her immediate thought was still to refuse the bequest. She didn't want to take anything from Douglas. If she took it, then she was taking money from a man who had treated her so appallingly she'd faked her own death to escape him.

The sound of the kitchen door opening made Evie start, and she looked up to see Violet staring at her.

'Are you all right?' The older woman hurried towards Evie, a concerned expression on her face.

Evie forced a smile and stood up. 'Yes, I'm fine. Just having a think for a moment, that's all.'

Violet raised an eyebrow, her shrewd eyes studying Evie from behind her horn-rimmed glasses. 'Well, you don't look it, and whatever you were thinking about has drained your face of colour.' She took hold of Evie's elbow. 'Come on.' Violet led her towards the sitting room, pausing in the kitchen doorway to call in to Thea, 'Can you make a cup for Evie, too? Put some sugar in it. I'm taking her to sit down.'

Settled in an armchair, Evie sat looking at her hands clasped on her lap, aware that Violet was watching her from her seat on the settee. She only looked up at the sound of Thea coming in carrying a tray.

'This is the one with sugar in.' Thea put the tray down on a side table, and handed a cup of tea to Evie, then one to Violet, before taking one for herself and sitting down next to her friend. 'Did you make your telephone call?'

Evie nodded and took a sip of tea, its unaccustomed sweetness hitting her taste buds.

'What's happened?' Thea said.

'I've had some unwelcome news.' Evie cradled her cup in her hands. The warmth seeping into her fingers was comforting. 'The letter I received the other day was from Douglas's solicitor. It was to inform me that Douglas had left me a bequest in his will. But I don't want it.'

'Who's Douglas?' Violet asked.

'My late husband. He was a bully who physically hurt and belittled me. I faked my own death and ran away to escape from my marriage,' Evie explained in a flat tone.

Violet's eyes widened in horror. 'I'm sorry he treated you so terribly.' She leaned across and touched Evie's arm. 'Is that how you came to live here at Rookery House?'

Evie nodded. 'I'd trained in secret to become a VAD and worked in a hospital in London after Douglas was sent overseas with the army. During the Blitz, I witnessed how a young woman completely disappeared after a direct hit by a bomb. There was nothing left but her handbag.' She paused for a moment. 'It made me think I could pretend to disappear like that and Douglas would never know. It didn't matter in the end as he was killed in North Africa and won't be coming back. I'm free of him now, only…' Evie let out a heartfelt sigh. 'It seems that even in death he has the power to reach out to me…' Her voice tailed off as she gave a shudder.

'You've done marvellously to rebuild a life for yourself,' Thea said.

'I was very lucky coming to live here. It has helped me a lot.' Evie gave her friend a grateful smile. 'I was happy until that letter turned up. It's stirred up awful memories of my marriage again.' She shook her head. 'I got into trouble yesterday at work because it was weighing on my mind so much I wasn't concentrating. I had to find out what the letter was about or it would have kept gnawing away at me.'

'Now you know, what are you going to do?' Violet asked.

Evie chewed on her bottom lip. 'My first reaction is to not accept it. It's five thousand pounds, as Douglas left most of his money to his parents.'

'Five thousand pounds!' Thea and Violet chorused.

Evie nodded. 'It's still a lot, but even so… it feels like blood money to me.'

Violet leaned forwards, her eyes fixing on Evie's. 'I understand your reluctance to take *anything* from a man who hurt you, but with the wisdom of years, I caution you not to make any hasty decision which you may later come to regret. In my opinion, after the way you were treated, you deserve that money, Evie. Take it, put it in the bank and if you don't want to spend any, then leave it there and do not touch it for the time being. One day you might come to be glad about having it. It could buy you a house, make you secure with somewhere to live. Or you might decide you never want it and could give it away to an orphanage or something, use it to do some good with, help others. Just don't do anything hasty now.'

'Violet's right,' Thea agreed. 'You're in shock and it's stirred up terrible memories, but that money could help you in the future.'

Evie looked at the two older women. Hearing their argument for accepting the money and tucking it away for the future made sense. She nodded. 'You're right. I need to detach how I feel about Douglas from the money. I'll take it and put it in the bank and forget about it. It will be there *if* I ever need it or decide what to do with it.'

'That's a wise decision. To be honest, I think after what Douglas put you through, he owes you that money,' Thea said.

Evie lifted a shoulder. 'Perhaps. I don't want to tell anyone else about this. Please don't say anything to the others. I'll put it in the bank and forget about it. Get on with my life again.'

'Of course, I won't say a word,' Thea promised.

'Nor will I,' Violet added. 'I hope you feel better for having decided about it?'

'I do.' Evie managed a smile. 'I want to get back to normal again. Put Douglas firmly in the past where he belongs.'

CHAPTER 11

'The last time we were out driving around like this together was in an ambulance in France,' Violet said.

Thea glanced at her friend, who sat next to her in the cab of the WVS canteen. 'At least we haven't got any injured soldiers in the back this time.'

Normally, it would have been Thea's sister, Prue, sitting beside her. But Prue had a heavy cold and wasn't well enough to do her shift, so Violet had volunteered to fill her place instead. Now they were on their way to various scattered military outposts to provide the servicemen and women stationed at them with a chance to buy food, drinks and a selection of goods.

'Back then, we never thought the world would be at war again just twenty-odd years later,' Violet said in a sombre tone. 'And yet here we are. Only this time it has had a bigger impact on the home front. It isn't mostly taking place out of sight in foreign lands.'

'The Great War was supposed to be *the war that ended all*

wars.' Thea shook her head. 'I wish it had been.' She let out a weary sigh. 'Listen to us, there's no point in getting maudlin. It won't alter anything.' She glanced at Violet. 'I'm glad you've come out with me today, even though you should be resting on your holiday.'

'I'm enjoying myself. And a change is as good as a rest, as they say. This is a chance for me to see more of your beautiful Norfolk countryside.' Violet waved her hand at the view out of the windscreen. 'I've had plenty of cups of tea from WVS canteens in London, so it's interesting to be on the other side doing the serving, discovering how it all works. I'll be able to tell the crew about it when I get back to Station 75.'

'You're about to find out.' Thea braked gently as they approached the turning to the searchlight detachment, which was one of the regular WVS canteen stops. 'That's our first stop up ahead.'

A few minutes later, parked on the grassy field by the detachment, Thea and Violet had moved into the back of the canteen and were busy preparing to open for business.

'It's so well organised in here,' Violet said as she dropped cubes of red tomato soup concentrate into one of the urns. 'There's a place for everything and everything in its place. It's a clever design keeping things safe while you're moving.' She waved her hand at the slide-out drawer, with its individual storage compartments, from which Thea was taking cups and setting them on the counter, ready to use.

'I'm sure your ambulances are well organised too,' Thea said, glancing at her friend who, like herself, was wearing a green apron with WVS embroidered in red on the chest pocket.

'Yes, I suppose they are, but not in quite the same way as

this canteen. There's not so much room in them, with most of the space being taken up with the stretchers on the frames, but we make the best use of what we have,' Violet said. 'What shall I do next?'

'You can put those cheese and potato pies in the oven to warm through,' Thea instructed, carrying on with her preparations. 'Are you missing being at Station 75?'

Her friend closed the oven door, after putting the pies inside it to heat, and considered for a moment before replying. 'Yes and no!' She gave a short laugh. 'That's not a very satisfactory answer, is it?'

The corners of Thea's mouth curled up in amusement as she glanced at her friend. 'Perhaps not, but I'd say that's a very *Violet* sort of answer! Tell me what makes it a yes *and* a no?'

Violet turned to face Thea. 'Well, I'm delighted to be here spending time with my dear friend and to have the chance to recuperate with some peace and quiet in the beautiful Norfolk countryside. On the other hand, I do miss knowing what's going on back at Station 75. I would love to know how Winnie is getting on. If she's keeping everything as it should be in my absence.'

'But you've told me Winnie's quite capable of being in charge for a while, haven't you?'

'I have. And I wouldn't leave her to do the job if I didn't think she could. She has a good solid team around her, and they know the routines like the back of their hands. Thankfully the air raids have stopped for now, so Winnie hasn't got the pressure of organising who goes out when and to what.' Violet fell silent for a moment, her forehead creasing. 'For me, that's the hardest part of the job because I could unwittingly send a crew out to be injured or even to their deaths…' Her voice caught and she halted.

Thea saw that Violet's face had gone pale. Her brown eyes

were glistening with tears behind her horn-rimmed glasses. Thea put a hand on her friend's arm. 'Violet? Are you all right?'

Violet managed a watery smile. 'That's the part I find *most* challenging out of everything I do as a station officer. *I* make the choice, no one else. It was me who sent the Jones sisters out to an incident the night they were killed. If I'd chosen somebody else to go, then they all might still be alive.'

Thea's heart ached in sympathy for her friend. 'But it wasn't *your* fault they were killed. You didn't drop the bomb on them,' she said in a gentle voice, recalling the letter brimming with anguish that Violet had written to her after the two Jones sisters had been killed back in the early days of the Blitz. Clearly their deaths still weighed heavily on her friend.

Violet nodded. 'I know that. Logic tells me that. But my heart says otherwise. I was lucky that night not to lose the other two crews I sent out to the same incident. They took a different route to the Jones sisters, so they survived.'

'Doesn't that show you that chance, luck or whatever you call it, plays its part in whether or not somebody survives an air raid? Remember what it was like in France? We had several near misses from stray shells, didn't we? And we lost some friends who weren't so lucky.'

'We did.' Violet bit her bottom lip and then took in a deep breath. 'Look at me, I'm supposed to be on holiday getting away from it all and here I am confessing my worries and regrets to you. I'm sorry Thea.'

Thea took hold of Violet's hand in hers. 'There's no need to be sorry. You can tell me anything. In fact, it's good for you to talk about these things, so I'm glad you told me. I don't suppose you talk to many people about them. The responsibilities you have must weigh heavily on your shoulders.' Her eyes met Violet's and her friend gave a small nod of her head in acknowledgement. 'You've been through a terrible time with the Blitz. Don't be hard on yourself. You do a magnificent job running Station 75 and I know all the crew think highly of you. That sort of respect and admiration isn't easily won, so be proud of what you do.' Thea held Violet's gaze. 'I'm proud of you and of being your friend all these years.'

Violet blinked, her eyes glistening. 'Thank you. Fortune shone on me on the day we met. Now,' she raised her chin, 'those delicious looking pies smell like they're just about ready.' She sniffed at the savoury aroma that was filling the canteen. 'And, if I'm not mistaken,' she cocked her head to one side, listening, 'we already have some customers waiting outside.'

'We do indeed. They're always keen here.' Thea gave Violet a warm smile as she took some teaspoons out of a drawer and placed them on the counter for their customers to use. 'I'll open the hatch ready to do business in a minute. Can you get some of the chocolate bars, biscuits and fruit out of that cupboard please?'

Quickly finishing her own preparations, Thea was glad that Violet had talked about her worries. Throwing a glance at her friend, she saw Violet was looking better than she had earlier, as if a weight had been lifted off her. Thea knew that before this war was over, more worries would settle on Violet's shoulders from her demanding job, but at least for now, she had a bit of respite and her holiday was doing her good.

'Right, we're all set,' Thea said as she surveyed the counter laid out with filled bread rolls and other things to eat, ready for their customers. 'Prepare yourself for a busy time.'

Violet grinned. 'I'm all set.'

Thea nodded at her friend and then opened the hatch, the pair of them laughing as a chorus of cheers and clapping greeted them from the gathered servicemen and women waiting to be served.

CHAPTER 12

Marianne stood on the landing looking out through a window at the front of Rookery House, waiting for Alex to arrive. He had telephoned this morning to say that he'd been given a forty-eight-hour pass and was coming to whisk her and Emily away for two nights.

Excitement coursed through her veins at the prospect of seeing her husband again. With his life under the rule of the RAF, they saw so little of each other, only snatched visits when Alex was allowed some leave. This morning's unexpected telephone call from him had been a wonderful surprise. Marianne had planned to spend today working on the pattern for Lady Campbell-Gryce's new dress but had quickly shelved it to prepare for her and Emily's time away. Alex told her he'd booked for them to stay at a hotel not far from Wykeham. Now Marianne was packed, Emily was having her afternoon nap, and all they needed was for Alex to arrive.

The sound of an engine coming along the road raised Marianne's heart rate, but the sight of Alf Barker's grocery van trundling back from the direction of Great Plumstead Hall, heading towards the village, quickly dashed her hopes.

'Any sign of him?' Hettie's voice called from down in the hallway.

Marianne stepped away from the window and peered down to the bottom of the stairs, where Hettie stood looking up at her.

'Not yet, but I hope he'll be here soon. I'll keep watching out for him. I don't want to miss anything.'

'I've just made a pot of tea if you fancy a cup,' Hettie said.

'I'm fine, thank you,' Marianne replied.

'Fair enough.' The older woman gave her an understanding smile. 'It's there if you change your mind.' She headed back into the kitchen.

Marianne resumed her post by the window, watching and waiting.

As the aerodrome was over a hundred miles away Alex had only been able to give her a vague time of when to expect him since he couldn't be sure how long his journey would take. Marianne knew she could be using this time to get on with some sewing or another task, but she was far too excited to concentrate on anything. She wanted to wait, watch him arrive and not waste a moment when she could see him because each second was so precious.

It was just before three o'clock when a red sports car turned in at the gateway of Rookery House. Marianne pulled up the sash window and waved out of it, attracting Alex's attention. He looked up at her and beamed.

'Hello, darling,' he shouted up to her, climbing out of the car.

'I'll be right down,' she called back, before quickly closing the window, and hurrying down the stairs.

'He's arrived then!' Hettie said in an amused tone as

Marianne dashed through the kitchen towards the outside door.

'At last!' Marianne threw her friend a quick grin and bolted out of the door and around to the front of the house.

She met Alex coming the other way, and he scooped her up in his arms and off her feet, twirling her around before gently placing her on the ground and kissing her tenderly.

'Let me have a look at you.' He stood back, his conker-brown eyes dancing with happiness. Drinking her in, a wide smile settled on his face. 'You are so beautiful, Marianne. And…' he gently placed his hand on her rounded belly, 'you are positively blooming.'

Marianne laughed. 'I'm certainly bigger than last time you saw me.'

'Pregnancy suits you, darling. Truly, you look wonderful and I'm so happy to be here with you.' Alex put his arm around her. 'Where's Emily?'

'She's having a nap, but should be waking up soon, or she won't sleep tonight. Shall we go and see if she is awake?'

Alex nodded. 'I can't wait to see her.'

Upstairs in the bedroom Marianne shared with her daughter, she pulled the curtains open, allowing the October afternoon sunlight to stream in, hoping that it would gradually stir Emily from her nap.

'She's beautiful, just like her mother.' Alex gently stroked Emily's sleep-flushed cheek. 'She has grown since I last saw her. Every time she's that bit bigger.' He sighed, glancing at Marianne. 'I'm missing so much being away from you both. Once the war is over, we can all be together as a proper family.'

She went over to him and put her arms around his waist. 'We miss you too.'

Emily's eyes opened, then closed, her dark eyelashes fluttering against her creamy skin. Then suddenly her eyes snapped open, obviously having registered who was standing beside her cot.

'Dadda!' Emily scrambled to her feet by the bars of the cot and held out her arms to Alex. 'Dadda.'

'Hello my darling.' Alex picked her up and cuddled her to him. 'She remembers me,' he said, his eyes meeting Marianne's, a joyful smile lighting his face.

'Of course she does. We say goodnight to your photograph at bedtime, don't we, Emily?' Marianne gestured towards the framed picture of Alex standing on the nightstand beside her bed. 'We might not see you as much as we would all like, but we certainly haven't forgotten you.'

Emily was perfectly content in Alex's arms and was playing with the gold buttons on his air force blue RAF tunic.

'Are you ready to go?' he asked. 'I told the hotel to expect us any time after three o'clock.'

'We're all packed.' Marianne gestured towards the two suitcases that stood by the wardrobe. 'I just need to change Emily and give her a drink and then we can be on our way.'

'Excellent.' Alex leaned across and kissed Marianne's cheek. 'We won't have room for the pram this time. The only car I could borrow was Smithy's Alvis Tourer, but I thought now Emily's walking we could do without it for a couple of days. If she gets tired, then I'll carry her.'

'I'm sure we'll manage and it will be fine.' Marianne held out her arms. 'Let me take Emily and get her freshened up and we can soon be on our way.'

❧

The hotel was warm and welcoming. After a delicious meal in the dining room where a roaring fire kept the chill of the autumn evening at bay, Marianne and Alex went up to their room. Emily was already sleeping in the cot, having had her meal earlier. Alex had read her a story before her eyes had drooped and she'd fallen asleep in his arms.

'I can't tell you how wonderful it feels to be with you both,' Alex said, gazing down into Marianne's eyes as he put his arms around her. 'We might not be together much in reality, but in my heart and my head, you are *always* with me.'

Tears prickled the back of Marianne's eyes and she fought hard to suppress them. She didn't want to spoil this moment by getting upset.

'I feel the same. You are with us in here.' She laid a hand over her heart. 'When I woke up this morning, I thought it was going to be another normal day, but your phone call transformed it.' She gave him a radiant smile. 'And look where we are now, together at last.'

Alex raised an eyebrow. 'Let's make the most of it, then!' He lowered his head and kissed her.

CHAPTER 13

'It brings it home how widespread this war is,' Flo said as the Pathé News reel came to an end.

'Watching the news on film where you can see real people has much more impact than reading about it in a newspaper,' Evie agreed.

The image of British troops in the desert had been a sobering one, especially as Alice's brother Edwin was somewhere out there driving ambulances for the Friends Ambulance Unit. The tentacles of war and its destruction of people's homes and lives had spread far and wide. And there was still no sign of the end in sight and going from what they'd seen on the news reel, it was a long way off.

'I'm ready to be whisked away by the film after that,' Evie said.

'So am I,' Alice said, with a sigh, the images clearly having affected her.

'Are you all right?' Flo asked.

'Yes.' Alice managed a smile. 'I'm just nipping out to the kiosk to get some sweets before the main film starts. I'll be two ticks.' She stood up from her seat next to Evie, which was at the end of the row, and hurried off to the foyer.

'She probably needs a moment,' Evie said to Flo.

Evie had come to the pictures in Wykeham tonight with Flo and Alice, making the most of her monthly weekend off from her duties at the hospital. This was her second visit to the town today, as Mr Willoughby had sent her a cheque for her bequest from Douglas, and she'd bicycled into the town this morning to deposit it in her account at the bank. Evie still had no idea what she would do with the money, or even if she would use it or simply give it away later. For now, it would sit in her account while she got on with her life. She was so grateful that Douglas was no longer part of her world and she was free to do as she wished.

Coming here with two of the friends she'd made since going to live at Rookery House, Evie thought about how much her life had changed for the better. She couldn't help smiling.

'What are you looking so happy about?' Flo asked.

'That I'm here tonight, with you and Alice.' Evie leaned her head closer to Flo and lowered her voice. 'Not so long ago, when I was with Douglas, I would never have been *allowed* to come out to the pictures with friends. After I'd been with him a little while, I didn't have any friends left to go out with. He'd discouraged me from having any contact with the friends I'd made at school who he didn't consider acceptable and, sadly, they drifted away. He only allowed me to socialise with people he approved of.'

'I'm sorry he did that to you. It wasn't right.' Flo put a hand on Evie's arm. 'Would he have approved of me do you think?'

'Oh no!' Evie gave a brief laugh.

'Good,' Flo said firmly.

Evie's gaze met Flo's in the dim light. Her friend was one

of the few people in Great Plumstead who knew about Evie's past and how terribly Douglas had treated her.

'But after going through that it makes the life I have now so much the sweeter. Being able to come here tonight without having to ask anyone's permission is wonderful. It is so liberating.'

'I can imagine. And especially if it's to see a film of one of your favourite books,' Flo said, as the opening credits of *Pride and Prejudice* appeared on the screen in front of them and the stirring music filled the picture house.

'Definitely, and particularly with the handsome Laurence Olivier playing Mr Darcy,' Evie agreed.

'Just in time,' Alice said, slipping into her place beside Evie. 'Here, have a mint humbug.' She offered the open bag of sweets for them to help themselves.

'Thank you,' Evie said, taking a humbug and popping it into her mouth, the sweet mintyness tingling refreshingly on her tongue. She settled back into her red, plush fabric seat with a sigh of contentment and focused her full attention on the screen in front of her.

CHAPTER 14

'On a day like this, there's something wonderfully cosy about toasting home-made crumpets on an open fire,' Violet said, glancing at the rivulets of rain running down the half-glass doors of the sitting room at Rookery House which overlooked the back garden. She returned her gaze to the crumpet speared on the end of the metal toasting fork which she was holding in front of the hot flames of the fire.

'You might not want to go back to London tomorrow,' Hettie said, who was sitting in an armchair by the fireside, her fingers moving in a blur as she worked on the blue sock she was knitting.

'You're welcome to stay longer,' Thea added, from where she sat, like Violet, on a small stool in front of the fire, toasting her own crumpet.

'I wish I could. My week here has gone by so fast.' Violet removed the crumpet from the end of her long fork, turned it round and re-speared it to toast the other side, working quickly to avoid burning her fingers. 'But I'm due back on duty at Station 75 tomorrow night. It's been such a treat to be here.' She looked at Thea and gave her a grateful smile. 'I've thoroughly enjoyed myself.'

A burst of laughter came from the kitchen where Evie and Flo were playing a game of snakes and ladders with George and Betty.

'Even though you've been put to work at times!' Hettie chuckled.

'Oh, but I've enjoyed all of it,' Violet declared. 'I'd never milked a cow until Thea taught me how to milk Primrose. Going out on the WVS canteen was an eye-opener. Those canteens are so cleverly designed, and I had no idea they provided such an essential service for troops stationed out in the countryside miles from the nearest shop or cafe.'

'They certainly do. The servicemen and women rely on us to visit them,' Thea said as she removed a completely toasted crumpet from her fork and placed it on the plate by the fire, then re-covered it with a tea cloth to keep those already toasted warm. Then she threaded another crumpet on her toasting fork and began the process all over again.

The sitting-room door opened and Marianne came in. 'Emily's down for her afternoon nap at last. The past few days away with Alex have worn her out but sometimes, the more tired she is, the harder it is for her to let go and sleep!' She sat down in the armchair opposite Hettie and leaned back into it with a sigh. 'It's lovely to sit down by the fire and relax. I ought to be getting on with Lady Campbell-Gryce's dress but...'

'You need to rest, Marianne,' Thea said. 'The dress can wait.'

'Thea's right,' Hettie agreed, in a firm voice. 'And there's hot buttered crumpets to be had shortly, if you want some!'

Marianne smiled at the older woman. 'That's an offer I'm not going to turn down.'

'They're perfect for a day like this,' Violet said. 'I must get some to toast at Station 75. I'm sure they'd go down a treat with the crews.'

'Do you think, if you were still living in London, Thea, that you'd have joined the ambulance service for the duration?' Marianne asked.

Thea thought for a moment before replying, 'Possibly, in fact, probably if Violet had encouraged me to join. It could have been like old times working together.'

'I would have loved to have worked with you again.' Violet put her hand on Thea's shoulder. 'There's always a job for an experienced and excellent ambulance driver like you at Station 75 if you want it.'

'Thank you, but my days of living in London are over. Besides, I still get to drive ambulances occasionally for the WVS and put my experience to good use.' Thea quickly turned the crumpet she was toasting over to do the other side.

'I remember you learning to drive,' Hettie said, her eyes twinkling in amusement behind her round glasses. 'How the chauffeur, who was sweet on you, taught you in Lord Campbell-Gryce's motor car!'

'Is that true?' Marianne asked.

Thea nodded. 'I was working as a kitchen maid at the Hall and Hettie was assistant cook then. And yes, the chauffeur did teach me to drive in his Lordship's car. It was a miracle we never got found out by anyone who'd report what we were doing to the Campbell-Gryces. Otherwise, we'd both have been thrown out of a job.'

Marianne leaned forward in her chair. 'How did he manage to teach you, then?'

'It was when the Campbell-Gryce's were staying at their house in London. And I only drove on quiet roads well away from the estate, so there was less likelihood of being seen.

Luckily, I learned quickly and then I volunteered to drive ambulances in France, and that's when I met Violet.' She smiled at her friend. 'We both arrived on the same day and have been friends ever since.'

'It was highly unusual for someone who worked as a kitchen maid to learn to drive,' Hettie said. 'But look where it took you and ultimately led you here to Rookery House.' She gestured with her hand.

Thea nodded. 'I suppose it did. Taking that risk to learn changed the direction of my life.'

The door to the sitting room burst open and George and Betty raced in.

'George won,' Betty announced, 'and I came second! Are the crumpets ready?'

'Just about,' Thea said. 'Only these two left to toast.' She indicated the ones on each end of hers and Violet's toasting forks.

'I love toasted crumpets,' George said, coming to stand beside Thea. He put his arm around her shoulder and gave her a sideways hug. 'Thank you for making them.'

Thea hugged him back with her free arm. 'You're welcome. Now, why don't you and Betty go through to the kitchen and tell Evie and Flo the crumpets are almost done and to get the plates and knives ready, and the butter, jam and honey out of the pantry, and we'll bring them through in a jiffy.'

The two children hurried off to do as they were asked.

'They didn't need telling twice,' Violet said, removing the crumpet from her toasting fork and placing it under the cloth with the others already toasted.

Thea laughed. 'They never do where crumpets are concerned. You might find if you toast some at Station 75, they'll have a similar effect!'

'Then I definitely need to get some,' Violet replied.

'That's the last one done.' Thea removed the crumpet from her toasting fork and added it to the pile under the cloth, then stood up and carried the plate into the kitchen, the others following behind ready to enjoy Hettie's delicious home-made crumpets, topped with creamy butter and perhaps some jam or honey as the mood took them.

CHAPTER 15

'Are you sure you're happy to look after Emily?' Marianne asked as she climbed out of the car Lady Campbell-Gryce had sent to bring them to Great Plumstead Hall.

'Of course I am. We're going to visit Auntie Ada, aren't we?' Hettie said, directing her question to Marianne's young daughter who stood holding Hettie's hand, looking wide-eyed around her at the tall, impressive facade of the Hall.

'Thank you. Please send for me if you need me to come and get Emily,' Marianne said.

'We'll be fine,' Hettie reassured her.

'Ada and Dorothy are looking forward to seeing you and the little girl,' the chauffeur said, closing the car door, which he'd held open for them. 'Dorothy's been doing lots of baking ready for the afternoon tea.'

Marianne gave him a smile. 'Then I'm sure they'll have a lovely time.'

'Can I carry your basket in for you?' the chauffeur asked, nodding at the basket Marianne was holding.

'No, I'm fine. Thank you for bringing us,' Marianne said.

The chauffeur touched the brim of his peaked cap. 'You're welcome. Just send word when you've finished and I'll take you home again.'

They made their way round to the west wing of the Hall where Marianne would be doing a fitting of Lady Campbell-Gryce's dress.

Upstairs in her Ladyship's dressing room, Marianne watched as the older woman turned this way and that, regarding her reflection in the long cheval mirror.

'It's perfect! Fits like a glove.' Lady Campbell-Gryce ran her hands over the soft, wine-red velvet that skimmed over her slim figure. 'You've done an excellent job, Marianne.'

'Thank you, I just need to check the hem to make sure it's exactly as we want it.' Marianne knelt on the floor beside her Ladyship, checking around the bottom of the skirt, using her tape measure to ensure it was the same length from the waist all the way round.

Marianne was pleased with how the dress had turned out, although it had taken her longer to make than it would have done in the past, but back then, she hadn't had a small child to care for as well as being pregnant. Over the last three weeks, since she'd returned from her all too brief time away with Alex, Marianne had worked on it whenever she could. First, she had finalised the design, making a pattern and had done a couple of previous fittings with her Ladyship. Today was the final one, and if everything was perfect, then the work with this dress was finished.

'The hem looks fine. It's straight and exactly as it should be.' Marianne got to her feet and cast her eye critically over the rest of the dress, checking the seams and the fit. There was nothing she could see that needed altering or improving. 'That's it, it's ready,' she declared. 'You look lovely in it. The colour suits you perfectly.'

'Thank you, but it's all due to your incredible flair with design and tailoring. I am so lucky to be able to use your skills to turn *curtains* into something so beautiful and wearable.' Lady Campbell-Gryce gave Marianne an appreciative smile. 'Who'd have thought this dress was made from an old pair that had been tucked away and forgotten in a trunk in the attic? It's a perfect example of making do for the war effort.'

'I'm glad you like it. I enjoyed working on it.'

Lady Campbell-Gryce went over to her dressing table, opened a drawer, took out an envelope and handed it to Marianne. 'There's extra in there than the fee you agreed. Please accept it with my thanks. I know you have far less time to devote to your dressmaking these days and I appreciate you fitting me in.'

'Thank you.' Marianne took the envelope and put it in her handbag.

'Now, if you would be so good as to undo the buttons on the back, then I'll change into my everyday clothes. Would you like to join me for some afternoon tea?'

'I'd like that very much, thank you,' Marianne replied as she began to undo the small buttons.

Downstairs in Lady Campbell-Gryce's sitting room, as Marianne helped herself to some sandwiches from a delicious looking spread of afternoon tea, her Ladyship began to talk about her daughter Cecilia.

'She has been posted to Scotland and is ferrying naval

officers around. She says the weather is quite shocking at times,' Lady Campbell-Gryce explained.

Marianne had enjoyed hearing about Cecilia's exploits as a Wren driver from Lady Campbell-Gryce during their earlier dress fittings, as it was all thanks to Cecilia that Marianne was now married to Alex.

'Is she still happy with her work?' Marianne asked, before taking a bite of potted meat sandwich.

'Absolutely. I think she's having a wonderful time.' Her Ladyship laughed. 'Cecilia always makes the best of everything.' She took a sip of tea and lowered her cup back onto its bone china saucer. 'I was wondering, Marianne, would you be able to make me a blouse? If you remember there was a particularly nice Nottingham lace tablecloth, and I have an old silk nightgown that would work as a lining underneath it. What you think? Could you squeeze it in for me?' Her Ladyship's blue eyes fixed on Marianne's. 'There would be no rush, whenever you can manage it.'

Marianne considered for a moment. Lady Campbell-Gryce was a loyal customer. If she was willing to wait then Marianne would enjoy working with the high-quality fabric. 'I'd be delighted to, as long as I can fit it in when I can. It's impossible to give you a deadline when it will be ready by.'

'Thank you!' Lady Campbell-Gryce said in a grateful voice. 'I *love* the way we're turning old and used items into something so wonderful and wearable. Shall we talk about the design while you're here?'

'Of course, what were you thinking of?' Marianne asked, reaching for her handbag and taking out her notebook.

CHAPTER 16

Wrapped up well in her warm greatcoat, scarf and gloves, Evie was enjoying being outside on a crisp November morning with its blue sky arching high overhead. Low temperatures last night had dusted the world in frost and patches of it remained in the shadows where the pale winter sun had failed to reach.

'We'd better start heading back to the hospital, or you'll be late for your midday meal and Matron will be on the warpath,' Evie said, as she pushed Private Howard along in his wheelchair.

'Fair enough. We don't want to upset Matron. I've noticed she can be mighty scary when she's riled,' Private Howard replied. Like Evie, he was warmly dressed as well as being tucked under a thick layer of soft woollen blankets.

Evie laughed. 'She certainly is, but she is an excellent Matron nonetheless and keeps the hospital running smoothly. She's the reason you're out here this morning. Matron's a great believer in the restorative powers of fresh air.'

'I'm grateful to her as it's good to get outside again,' Private Howard said.

Skirting the tall red brick walls of the kitchen garden, Evie steered the wheelchair towards the terrace at the back of the Hall. What had once been an expanse of closely cropped green lawn had been dug up to create large vegetable beds to grow more food to use in the hospital. It was all part of the government's drive to Dig for Victory. Where the Campbell-Gryce's probably once played croquet, there now grew a wide array of vegetables.

Evie spotted a gardener pushing a wheelbarrow heading towards them from the opposite direction. It was a man that she hadn't seen here before wearing round glasses, the sunlight glinting off them, but there was something familiar about him, Evie thought, as they drew closer. With a start, she realised who it was, and she halted, her stomach leaping in surprise.

'Ned?' she called. 'What are you doing here?'

Ned Blythe, known as Private Blythe the last time he was here at Great Plumstead Hall Hospital, strode towards her with a delighted smile on his face.

'Hello Evie, I've been hoping to see you. I'm the new gardener,' he explained. 'Ned Blythe.' He held out his hand to Private Howard. 'I was a patient here earlier this year before I was medically discharged from the army.'

Private Howard shook hands. 'And now you've come back.'

'I have,' Ned replied, his gaze briefly settling on Evie, before returning his attention to the injured soldier. 'It's a nice place, and when the offer of this gardening job came up, I couldn't turn it down.'

'How long have you been here and why didn't you tell me you were coming?' Evie asked.

'I arrived yesterday and started work this morning. I didn't say anything to you because I wanted to surprise you. That's why I haven't written to you for a couple of weeks. I didn't trust myself not to give the game away,' Ned said. 'I wrote to Lady Campbell-Gryce in the summer asking her to let me know if she ever had any gardening jobs going and she wrote back to me last month and offered me a job, and here I am.' He gestured with both his hands. 'It's good to be back.'

'I wondered why I hadn't heard from you. Where are you staying?' Evie asked.

'I'm lodging with Mr White, the head gardener, and his wife, in their cottage on the estate,' Ned explained.

Evie's eyes met his, and they stared at one another for a moment before she recovered herself. 'It's good to see you and I hope you'll enjoy your job.'

'I'm sure I will. And I'd better get on with it.' Ned gave her a warm smile, his eyes lingering on her for a few moments before he headed off, pushing the wheelbarrow in the direction they'd come from.

As Evie watched him go, she mused on her reaction at seeing him. She'd been pleased, perhaps more than that...

'Are you as happy to see him back as he was to see you?' Private Howard asked, a grin breaking out on his face.

'Of course, I was glad to see Ned again. He was one of my patients and we kept in touch after he left and was discharged from the army.'

'Do you do that with all your patients, then?' Private Howard asked.

She shook her head. 'Well, no. But we both love books and that's what we mostly write about. When Ned arrived here back in January, his eyes were bandaged over so I read to him because he couldn't see. After his bandages were removed, it took a while for his eyesight to be good enough for him to read himself, so I carried on. We share a love of books and reading, that's all.'

Private Howard raised an eyebrow. 'If you say so, but if you ask me,' he lowered the tone of his voice, 'Ned isn't just interested in what books you've been reading!'

Evie's cheeks grew warm. 'I can assure you, Private Howard, that we are just friends with a mutual appreciation of good literature,' she said in a firm voice. Without waiting for him to respond, she took hold of the handles of the wheelchair again and pushed him back towards the hospital.

Whatever Private Howard thought, he was wrong, Evie told herself. And besides she would *never* allow herself to pursue a relationship with a man again, other than a platonic friendship. After what she'd been through with Douglas, it was absolutely the right path to take. And the safest. She wasn't going to risk becoming entangled in another unhappy relationship. Ever!

CHAPTER 17

Thea was on WVS duty. Instead of doing her usual role of driving the mobile canteen, she'd been assigned the role of ambulance driver. She'd swapped her normal WVS uniform dress for a more practical pair of the service's green overalls and replaced the WVS felt hat with a red and white polka dot scarf tied around her brown curly hair.

'We'll soon have you inside and settled,' Thea said to Private Carey. He and the three other men they'd already carried inside had come from the main hospital in Norwich. They'd continue their recovery here at the quieter Great Plumstead Hall Hospital.

'Are you ready, Pat?' She directed her question to her fellow WVS worker, who she usually did ambulance duties with.

'All set,' Pat replied from where she stood outside the ambulance. 'On the count of three. One, two, three.'

They worked as a team gently gliding the stretcher out of its runners, then taking the weight of it to keep the patient as level as they could. Thea was grateful that she was strong, her physical work at Rookery House keeping her fit and able to carry laden stretchers.

Carrying their patient in through the front door of the hospital, they headed across the entrance hall to Dining Room Ward, where Matron Reed had instructed them to bring the patients when they'd first arrived.

The ward was busy with nurses settling the newcomers in, overseen by Matron, whose beady eyes didn't miss anything.

'Over there!' Matron ordered, waving Thea and Pat towards the empty bed by the window. 'Nurse Robertson and Nurse Jones, this patient needs transferring into his bed.'

Thea and Pat held the stretcher steady as Evie and the other nurse expertly moved the patient over.

'Thank you.' Private Carey gave a grateful smile.

'Get Private Carey settled,' Matron instructed, after a quick glance at the notes that had come with him. 'Then we can get you a nice cup of tea and something to eat,' she told the young man.

Matron turned to Thea and Pat. 'Thank you for your assistance. If you'd like to have a cup of tea yourselves before you leave, we can provide that for you in the kitchen.'

Thea glanced at Pat, who gave a nod of her head. 'Thank you, that would be lovely. I know where the kitchen is.'

'Jolly good.' Matron gave them a brief smile and then bustled off to the other end of the ward where she'd spotted something not to her liking and was swift to reprimand the poor nurse responsible.

Evie touched Thea's arm as she turned to leave. 'Can I speak to you before you go? I'll be coming down to the kitchen to get the tea for the new patients shortly. I won't be long.'

'Of course.' Thea gave her a smile, wondering what the young woman wanted to talk about. She'd thought Evie looked a bit unsettled, but then she was busy on the ward and with Matron Reed prowling around, it was enough to make anyone feel uncomfortable. 'I'll see you there.'

The kitchen of the hospital was warm and welcoming and the staff there had happily provided Thea and Pat with a cup of tea and a freshly baked biscuit each.

'I needed that!' Pat said, putting down her empty cup on the table and leaning against the back of the wooden chair.

They'd been sent to have their tea and biscuit in the large dining room where the mobile patients now came to eat. It had once been where the Hall's servants had eaten their meals and was quieter than the busy kitchen where the staff were preparing the next meal.

'Same here,' Thea agreed. She gazed around the room. 'I remember this place so well.'

'Of course, you used to work here,' Pat said.

'I did, a long time ago. It was my first job working as a kitchen maid. Hettie helped me get it as she was assistant cook then. I left to go and drive ambulances in France,' Thea explained.

'Now you are driving them again in another war and bringing patients here. Like coming full circle!' Pat said.

'Thea! Sorry to keep you waiting,' Evie said, hurrying into the room. 'I haven't got long, just while the kitchen staff get the tea and biscuits ready, but I wanted to speak to you…'

'You two have a talk.' Pat stood up. 'I'll meet you back at the ambulance, Thea.' She gathered their used cups and plates and headed off to the kitchen.

'Are you all right?' Thea asked, looking at Evie, who had plonked herself down in Pat's chair.

'I had a shock this morning.' Evie clasped her hands tightly together in her lap. 'Ned Blythe is here! He's got a job as a gardener and started work today.'

'Did you know he was coming to work here?'

'No, he hadn't written for a couple of weeks. I didn't know if he was ill or something. He said he wanted to surprise me. He did!'

Thea studied the young woman's face for a moment. She looked torn, as if she wasn't sure what to think. 'Was it a good surprise, or a bad one?'

Evie bit her bottom lip. 'A good one. I like Ned very much, it's lovely that he's here, and it's much better to see a friend in person than just write to them. Only...' Evie halted and twisted her mouth to the side.

'Only what?' Thea prompted.

'Well, when I saw him, it...' Evie shook her head. 'I don't know. But Private Howard, who I'd taken out for a walk in his wheelchair, made something of it. He said Ned looked very pleased to see me, more than just a friend would.'

'Did Ned look like that?'

Evie threw her hands in the air. 'I don't know! And it doesn't matter anyway, because I have no intention of ever getting involved that way with a man again.' Evie's voice was firm.

Thea reached out and touched the young woman's arm. 'I understand your reasons, but don't dismiss what could be a good thing because of the past. It would be a shame to miss out on something that could bring you much joy and happiness because of what happened with Douglas. It might or might not be with Ned, but one day you may find someone. Don't block yourself off for fear of what could happen. You're older, wiser and more experienced in life now and I think a far better judge of character.'

'I'm certainly older and had a lot of experiences, some of

which I never want to go through again. But I hope I'm wiser too.' Evie managed a smile. 'It's helped to talk about it. Ever since I saw Ned this morning it's been playing on my mind. I narrowly avoided a ticking off from Matron because I wasn't concentrating properly on what I was doing. Luckily, I spotted my mistake in time.'

Thea grinned. 'That was a lucky escape, then. Don't worry yourself about it. Just enjoy Ned being here as your friend. That's all you have to do. Think how wonderful it will be to share your love of books with him in person again.'

Evie smiled. 'Yes, you're right, that's what I need to focus on, nothing more.' She stood up. 'The men's tea must be ready now. Thank you, Thea.'

Thea got to her feet and put her arms around the young woman and gave her a hug. 'You're welcome. Any time you want to talk, you know where I am.'

Heading back to the ambulance, Thea couldn't help wondering if it was an auspicious thing that Ned Blythe had returned to Great Plumstead Hall Hospital to work in the gardens. At the very least, he was a good friend to Evie and who knew what it could lead to? Thea smiled to herself, thinking it would be lovely to see Evie happily settled with someone who loved and treasured her.

CHAPTER 18

Library Ward at Great Plumstead Hall Hospital was quiet this morning. Most of the patients who slept in here were mobile and had gone to spend time in the Recreation Room while the ward was being cleaned. It left just Private Chambers, who was still bed-bound. Evie, Hazel and Delia had been assigned the job of giving the ward a thorough clean by Matron Reed and were busy at work.

They never showed nurses doing these sorts of jobs on the posters advertising for women to become VADs, Evie thought as she washed the top of one of the lockers which stood beside each bed. It was a basic domestic task but an essential part of keeping the ward clean and hygienic. Evie didn't mind doing it, as it always gave her a sense of satisfaction at a job well done when she'd finished. But not all the VAD nurses shared her view, especially Delia, the newest recruit.

Evie threw a glance at Delia, who didn't look happy. Her face wore a bored expression as she half-heartedly washed a metal bed frame. Hazel, who was cleaning a bed further over, caught Evie's eye and gave a discreet nod towards Delia, raising her eyebrows, obviously thinking the same thing.

Abandoning her own work for a moment, Evie went over to Delia and crouched down beside her.

'How are you getting on?' she asked in a gentle voice.

Delia looked at Evie and rolled her eyes. 'Fine! It's only washing bed frames. It's not difficult, just absolutely boring and *not* want I want to be doing!' She pouted, her expression sulky.

'It isn't glamorous, I know, but it's important and must be done properly,' Evie said, ignoring the young woman's petulance. 'You need to make sure you wash *every* surface, clean in each corner and at the joins on the frame. Let me show you what I do.' She held out her hand to take the cloth from Delia. 'Make sure you rinse it out regularly.' She dunked the cloth in the bucket of water and disinfectant, swirled it around, then took it out and, as she wrung it out, the strong smell of carbolic hit her nose.

'This is how I do it.' Evie pulled the cloth between two of the upright metal bars on the headrest at the end of the bed frame, encased a bar completely in the material, and ran it up and down several times. Then she cleaned where it joined the horizontal bar at the bottom and the other end at the top, leaving no surface unwashed. 'If you do each part systematically, you won't miss any bits for Matron to find when she does her inspection later.'

Evie dropped the used cloth in the pail of disinfectant and stood up. 'All right?'

Delia looked up at her and nodded, before retrieving the rinsed cloth from the bucket, wringing it out with a heavy sigh and then starting again, this time doing as Evie had shown her. Delia didn't look any happier, but at least for the moment she was doing a better job.

Hazel gave Evie a quick thumbs up as she headed back to carry on with her own work.

As she washed down the side of the locker, Evie wondered if being a VAD really was the right job for Delia. Despite the young woman's enthusiasm when she'd arrived here six weeks ago, her progress had been slow. Much slower than any other VADs. Matron had kept Delia working on basic tasks like scrubbing out cupboards or preparing dressings to sterilise, along with frequent duties back in the sluice, until a few days ago. Now Matron had finally allowed Delia into the ward but only to do domestic cleaning jobs like this. As yet, Delia hadn't done any direct nursing of patients, which was exactly what she longed to do. Evie knew that until Delia could do the basic jobs properly and with a good heart, Matron Reed wouldn't progress her any further to work directly with the patients.

Evie, along with Hazel, was doing her best to guide Delia, but ultimately it was up to the young woman to help herself. A change in attitude would go a long way in helping her to succeed, Evie thought, but that could only come from Delia.

Evie and Hazel were on their way back to Library Ward carrying fresh pails of hot soapy water ready to wash the floor with. They'd finished cleaning the bedframes and lockers, then pushed the beds away from the walls into the middle of the ward. Delia had been given the simple job of sweeping the floors while they fetched the hot water.

'Do you think Delia will have done it properly?' Hazel asked in a low voice as they crossed the black and white tiled floor of the hall.

Evie glanced at her friend. 'I hope so. If not, she'll have to do it again. We won't be doing Delia any favours if we do it for her. She's got to learn to do it right herself.'

'I think…' Hazel began, but her voice tailed off as they reached the open door of Library Ward. They both halted at the sight of Delia sitting on the side of Private Chambers' bed listening to him talking and then bursting into giggles.

Evie quickly glanced behind her to check Matron wasn't heading their way and thankfully there was no one to be seen.

Evie plonked her pails down on the floor. 'Keep watch,' she instructed Hazel before dashing into the ward.

Delia, unaware of their return, said something to Private Chambers and burst into more giggles.

'Get up!' Evie grabbed hold of Delia's arm and pulled her to her feet. 'Nurses are *not* allowed to sit on patient's beds.'

Delia glared at Evie. 'I wasn't doing any harm! Private Chambers wanted a drink of water, and because he can't do it himself, I had to assist him.' She gestured towards his arms, which were both in plaster, making it impossible for him to help himself to either a drink or food. 'Then we just got chatting. Private Chambers must be getting bored having to stay in bed all day and with all of the other patients out in the Recreation Room this morning. I know I would be! It's good for him to have someone to talk to…'

'If Matron had come in and caught you sitting there,' Evie cut in. 'You'd have been back working in the sluice in a trice. She'd have kept you working in there until she decided otherwise. Matron's very strict about the *no sitting on beds* rule.'

'Well, I think it's a *silly* rule.' Delia folded her arms across her white apron, looking mutinous.

'Nurse Hastings wasn't doing any harm,' Private Chambers said, his face full of concern. 'It's true, I was thirsty and needed a drink. I was enjoying talking and having a laugh with her as well.'

'I appreciate that, Private Chambers, but Matron's a stickler for the rules and any nurse found sitting on a patient's bed is in *big* trouble. Take it from me, Matron would not have taken it lightly if she'd been the one to catch Nurse Hastings.' Evie turned to Delia. 'I'm trying to help you here, Delia, so don't go getting upset with me. Have you finished sweeping the floor?'

Delia's cheeks grew pink and she shook her head. 'I just was getting started when Private Chambers asked for a drink and...'

'Then you'd better get on with it. Do it quickly and properly. We've got pails of hot water cooling and a floor that needs scrubbing,' Evie said in a firm tone.

Delia didn't argue and retrieved the broom from where it lay abandoned on the floor and got to work.

Evie went to stand by Hazel, who stood on watch by the door. 'She's lucky it was us who caught her and not Matron.'

Hazel nodded, watching as Delia swept along one side of the ward under the windows. 'At the moment, she's more of a hindrance than a help. Matron's doing the right thing in keeping her from the patients until she's proved herself ready and capable. If she ever will be!'

Evie stood with Hazel on one side of her and Delia on the other, watching as Matron Reed made her inspection of Library Ward. They'd spent the last two hours working hard to finish the cleaning, down on their hands and knees scrubbing the floor before finally polishing it when it was dry. There was always the question whether it would pass Matron's exacting standards.

Hazel gave Evie's arm a small nudge as Matron finished

her usual inspection routine of running her finger along surfaces, and in nooks and crannies of places like bed frames to find any dirt. As she headed towards them, the look on Matron's face gave nothing away. Evie felt her heart rate increase as the older woman came to stand in front of them.

'You've done a satisfactory job. I can't find any dust or dirt anywhere,' Matron declared.

Evie sighed with relief inside but didn't dare express her feelings outwardly when she was facing Matron.

'Nurse Hastings, I want you back in the sluice until our midday meal and Nurse Robertson you can see to the laundry delivery,' Matron instructed in her soft Scottish no-nonsense voice.

Evie could sense Delia's dismay at being returned to working in the sluice, but thankfully she was sensible enough not to question Matron's order.

'Off you go then.' Matron nodded pointedly towards the door, and Hazel and Delia quickly left to carry out their next job.

Evie stood waiting, wondering what task Matron had in store for her.

'I understand that Private Blythe, as was, is now working here as a gardener,' Matron said, her gaze meeting Evie's.

'Yes, that's right. I met him in the garden when I was taking Private Howard for some fresh air a few days ago. It was Ned Blythe's first day working here,' Evie said.

Matron nodded and gave a slight smile. 'I would like to see him and hear how he's getting on. At two o'clock this afternoon, I want you to go and find Mr Blythe and ask him to come and have some tea with me. Bring him to my office with the tea things and *three* cups at three o'clock.'

'Yes Matron,' Evie said, doing her best to keep her face in a neutral expression and not show her surprise at these orders.

'Until then, you can prepare some more dressings to be sterilised,' Matron instructed before striding out of the ward.

Evie stood for a moment wondering what Ned would make of Matron's request to have tea with her. He was too polite to turn it down. And who else would be joining them? Perhaps Lady Campbell-Gryce as she had given him the job?

CHAPTER 19

At two o'clock Evie put on her coat, scarf and gloves and headed out into the chilly November afternoon to find Ned. Looking down from the terrace at the back of the hospital, she couldn't see him anywhere in the garden behind the house, so decided to try the walled garden.

Opening the wooden door and passing under the arched gateway was like stepping into another world. One where neat vegetable beds were laid out, and the walls were covered with espaliered fruit trees, though the branches were now bare of leaves. There was still no sign of Ned. Perhaps he was in the greenhouse or the bothy, both of which were on the far side of the kitchen garden built against one wall.

Approaching the bothy, Evie could hear men's voices and some laughing. She knocked on the wooden door and, not waiting for an answer, opened it and stepped inside. Ned was standing by a bench where some tools were laid out looking as if he were mending and cleaning them while Mr White, the head gardener, sat by the lit stove in an old threadbare armchair.

Ned looked surprised but delighted to see her and gave Evie a welcoming smile. 'Hello.'

'We have a visitor!' Mr White said, the stem of his unlit pipe clamped between his teeth. 'Not often we have a nurse come to see us. What brings you here?'

'Good afternoon,' Evie greeted him. 'I have a request for Ned from Matron Reed.'

Mr White raised his white bushy eyebrows, his expression wary. 'What does she want?'

Evie smiled to herself, thinking that Matron's fearsome reputation went way beyond the hospital wards. 'She wants Ned to join her for tea at three o'clock.' She turned to her friend. 'She's heard you're back and wants to know how you are.'

Ned's eyes widened in surprise. 'Really? I…'

'You *must* go lad, if a lady like Matron Reed asks you to take tea with her, then you'd best not say no.' Mr White chuckled. 'For your own sake, *and* mine!'

'But what about my work?' Ned asked, glancing at the tools laid on the bench.

'They'll still be there when you get back. I don't want Matron coming after me for not letting you go.' Mr White looked at Evie. 'It would be the wisest thing, don't you think, Nurse?'

'I agree.' Evie nodded before turning to Ned once more. 'Come to the kitchen at ten to three and I'll meet you there.' She glanced at his hands, which were covered with dark oily smudges. 'And make sure you give your hands a good wash beforehand. I think Lady Campbell-Gryce will be there.'

At her words, Mr White chuckled, leaning back in his chair. 'It's going to be an interesting afternoon for you lad, and no mistake.'

Evie had the tray with the tea things prepared as Matron had requested when Ned came into the kitchen right on time at ten minutes to three. She was pleased to see that he had done as she'd asked and his hands were clean. From the look of it, he'd even taken a comb to his brown hair and was now wearing a tweed jacket.

'Are you ready?' Evie asked, taking the kettle from the range and pouring hot water into the teapot.

'As I'll ever be.' Ned's face was wary. 'Do you know why she wants to see me?'

'All I know is what I told you. Matron said she wants to hear how you're getting on. She took a special interest in you while you were here before and I suppose it's rare to have a former patient return. She does care for her patients very much.'

Evie picked up the tray. 'Let's go, and don't look so worried. It won't be for long. If you can survive being on a battlefield, then you can easily manage having tea with Matron.' She gave him a cheeky grin then led the way out of the kitchen and headed towards Matron's office.

'I've got my hands full with this tray, so you'll have to knock,' Evie instructed Ned, after she'd checked the time on her nurse's watch pinned to her dress. It was exactly three o'clock.

Ned did as she asked and gave a tentative knock on the door of Matron's office.

'Come,' Matron Reed's voice called from within.

Ned took a deep breath, glanced at Evie, and opened the door. He then stood to the side and ushered Evie in.

'Mr Blythe!' Matron stood up from behind her tidy desk and came around to meet him.

Evie put the tray down on the desk and watched as Matron greeted Ned, taking his outstretched hand in both of hers and holding on to it while she looked him up and down.

'It's a delight to see you again.' Matron's voice was warm and welcoming. 'I must say you look extremely well and those glasses of yours suit you. Come and sit down.' Matron gestured to one of the two chairs set out in front of her desk. 'We'll have some tea, and you can tell me what you've been doing and what's brought you back to work here.'

As Ned sat down and Matron returned to her seat, Evie went to leave.

'Nurse Jones, shut the door and come and sit down. Who do you think the third cup is for if not for yourself?' Matron asked.

Evie managed to hold in her surprise. She hadn't expected to be included but knew better than to argue with Matron, even though taking tea with the older woman wasn't going to be comfortable. Why Matron wanted her there she didn't know, but knowing Matron she must have her own reason for it, because Evie could otherwise be busy doing some job around the hospital. She quickly shut the door and sat down next to Ned.

'So,' said Matron, pouring out three cups of tea. 'How are your eyes, Mr Blythe? Has there been any improvement since you left here?'

'A little. Not enough to pass me fit for the army, but I can see and I'm very grateful for that. There was a time when I thought I never would again.' Ned's voice was heartfelt.

'Milk?' Matron held up the little jug of milk and both Ned and Evie nodded. Matron added some to all three cups and then passed two across the desk towards her guests. 'We were all hopeful that you'd regain your sight, weren't we, Nurse Jones?' Matron turned her gaze to Evie.

'Yes, it was a nervous moment when your bandages were removed,' Evie said, as she took her cup of tea.

Matron nodded and focused her attention on Ned once more. 'As I recall, you were a chauffeur before the war. Did you not want to return to that line of work?'

'No, it wasn't for me any more. I wanted to be working outside and got a job in a garden, employed by a friend of my father's. I really enjoyed it. My father's a head gardener and I always thought his sort of job wasn't right for me, but to my surprise I was drawn to it.' He paused, looking thoughtful. 'Perhaps after what I went through, being outside in nature, working with the seasons, and taking the time to grow and nurture a garden was exactly what I needed. I remembered how much I liked the gardens here, when I could eventually see them. So I wrote to Lady Campbell-Gryce to ask if there was any chance of a gardening job. And here I am.'

'Indeed. I'm pleased to hear you have found a role that suits you so well. I am a firm believer that we should all do a job that we love.' Matron paused to take a sip of her tea, her eyes flicking from Ned to Evie and back again. 'I remember the day you left here, Mr Blythe, and your promise to write to Nurse Jones. Did you?'

Evie's cheeks grew warm. Was this why she'd been asked to stay?

Ned glanced at Evie briefly before turning to face Matron again. 'I did. We've been writing regularly ever since, continuing to share our love of books just as we did when I was here. I didn't tell Nurse Jones about accepting my job here though. I wanted to surprise her.'

Matron raised her eyebrows and turned her shrewd brown eyes on Evie. 'And were you surprised, Nurse Jones?'

'I was. I had no idea. When I saw Ned ... Mr Blythe working in the garden while I was taking Private Howard for a walk, it was a big surprise.'

'A pleasant one, I hope?' Matron probed, the corners of her mouth twitching.

'Yes, it was.' Evie glanced at Ned, who was watching her, and he gave her a smile.

'It will be easier to talk about books in person,' Ned said. 'I hope we can do that again.' His gaze met Evie's.

'Yes, I'd like that,' Evie said, forgetting for a moment that she was sitting in Matron's office under her beady eyes.

'That sounds like an excellent idea for you both,' Matron chimed in. 'Always good to stretch the mind by reading. Discussing it with a fellow book lover adds to the experience.' Her face creased into a wide smile.

Evie was startled for a few seconds. She had never seen the older woman look so pleased before.

'Now, Mr Blythe, tell me, what jobs has Mr White had you doing?' Matron asked, changing the subject.

Evie sipped her tea as Ned told Matron about his work. She was glad to fade into the background after Matron's startling and wholly unexpected encouragement that she and Ned should continue to see each other.

After a second cup of tea each, Matron glanced at her watch and stood up. 'I must get on. Thank you both for your company. It's been most pleasant and enlightening. I'm so pleased to see you back amongst us again, Mr Blythe and hope you will be happy in both your work and with your leisure time.' She gave him a beaming smile. 'Nurse Jones, if you could return the tray to the kitchen for me.'

'Of course.' Evie stood up, picked up the tray and followed

Ned to the door, which he held open for Matron to go through first.

Evie stepped out of the office and watched as Matron headed in the direction of the wards before she turned and led Ned back towards the kitchen.

'That wasn't too bad,' Ned said in a relieved voice. 'I quite enjoyed it. Did you mean what you said about getting together to talk about books? I miss writing letters to you, but it doesn't seem quite right to do it now when we're both in the same place again.'

Evie halted and looked at the man who'd become her unlikely friend all those months ago. 'I did, I miss your letters and writing back to you too. We need to work out when we can meet to talk properly, decide which book to read and discuss.'

'I'm reading the new Agatha Christie – *Evil Under the Sun*. I'll give it to you to read when I've finished. When could you meet?' Ned asked, his face hopeful.

'I get one day off a week, and it will often be when you're working. And one weekend a month, but my next weekend off isn't until the first week of December,' Evie explained.

'That's all right, we could have read a few books by then. I've got Ernest Hemingway's *For Whom the Bell Tolls* on order and will get it soon. We can both read that as well if you'd like. Maybe we could make a day of it, go to Wykeham and have a meal while we talk?'

Evie gave him a warm smile. 'I'd like that, thank you.'

CHAPTER 20

Marianne was kneeling by the bathtub, watching as Emily swirled the bubbles about on the surface of the warm water. Her daughter loved having a bath and enjoyed playing with the water, swooshing it around, making waves or dripping it from her fingertips.

'Five more minutes and then it's time to get out,' Marianne said, knowing that George and Betty would be next in the bath to make the most of the hot water which had been heated up in the copper ready for tonight's baths.

Leaning her elbow on the side of the bath, Marianne cupped her chin in her hand and joined in with the playing, drawing swirling patterns through the bubbly film on the water's surface with her fingers.

'Marianne,' Thea's voice called and she came into the bathroom. 'Alex is on the telephone for you.'

Marianne stared up at her friend in surprise. This wasn't one of his usual times to ring. Was something wrong?

'I'll take over here. You go and talk to him,' Thea said.

'Thank you.' Marianne stood up and hurried out of the

bathroom, through the scullery and into the kitchen, quickly drying her hand on her skirt. She wondered why Alex was telephoning now. Perhaps he had some unexpected leave, she thought, the prospect cheering her.

Reaching the hall, she paused for a moment and took a steadying breath before picking up the telephone receiver.

'Hello, Alex?'

'Darling!' As her husband's familiar voice came down the line, it sent a fluttering sensation looping around her stomach. 'How are you? And Emily?'

'We're both fine. Emily's in the bath. Thea's staying with her while I talk to you, otherwise she'd be here to say hello too. Are you all right?'

'Yes, of course, I just wanted to hear your voice,' Alex replied in a reassuring tone. 'I know I don't usually telephone at this time of day, but I couldn't wait until tomorrow. We're on an op tonight and I thought if I spoke to you before we go, then I'd be able to carry your voice with me.'

'I wondered if perhaps you had some leave,' Marianne said.

Alex sighed. 'If only. We had a wonderful time last month, didn't we? It was marvellous to be with you and Emily, even if it was just for two nights. Hopefully, it won't be too long before I get some more leave.'

'I hope so too,' she agreed. She could hear men's voices talking in the background. 'Where are you?'

'In the mess. Look, I'm going to have to go now as there's a line of other chaps wanting to use the telephone. It's been so good to talk to you, darling. Take care and give Emily a kiss for me.'

'I will. Alex, I…' she began, but he'd disconnected. Marianne slowly put the receiver back in its place, feeling strangely unsettled. He hadn't called because something was wrong, or even with news of some leave, but simply to speak to her. That was lovely, she supposed, so why had it left her with a gnawing sensation in the pit of her stomach?

Marianne shook her head, trying to dislodge the sense of disquiet that had settled over her. She was being silly, she told herself firmly. She should be delighted that Alex had telephoned unexpectedly, and she'd got to hear his voice and have some contact with him, no matter how distant and brief. That was something to be grateful for.

Right now, she had to get Emily out of the bath and ready for bed, though no doubt her daughter would protest at being removed from the water she loved so much. But it was Emily's bedtime and then Marianne wanted to do an hour's work on Lady Campbell-Gryce's blouse before she went to bed herself.

CHAPTER 21

Thea reached into the nest box and gently cupped her hand around the brown speckled egg and picked it up. It was still warm from the hen. She added it to the others she'd already collected in the straw-lined basket, making a total of six eggs laid this morning. The hens were laying much less frequently now than in the spring and summer months but were at least still providing them with far more eggs than most people got on the ration.

Closing the lid of the nest box, Thea glanced around the orchard where the hen coop was sited. She spotted Caesar, the cockerel, doing his best to keep his hens rounded up where he could see them. But as usual, they were ignoring him as they investigated grassy tussocks for insects and grubs or had a dust bath in the bare patch of soil under one of the apple trees. Thea laughed as she watched Caesar rushing this way and that, his magnificent bottle green, curved tail feathers blowing in the breeze.

Further down at the far end of the orchard, the white painted beehives stood quiet and still, waiting for warmer weather to arrive. The bees were hunkered down inside for the winter after a busy spring and summer's work. They'd produced a heavy crop of honey this year, which everyone at Rookery House enjoyed eating, and there'd been enough to sell some as well. The bees more than earned their keep, producing honey and pollinating so many of the crops they grew from the fruit trees to the beans and tomatoes.

Heading back to the house, walking past her brother Reuben's railway carriage house, Thea spotted Alice busy working in Five Acre Field. She was harvesting some winter vegetables to take into the village to supply Barker's grocery shop. Passing by the pigsty, Thea heard Flo inside the bedroom section talking to the piglets as she cleaned out their soiled bedding, adding it to the wheelbarrow that stood in the doorway.

Reaching the house, Thea went in through the door that led to the scullery, where she kicked off her muddy rubber boots and stood the basket of eggs by the sink so they could be washed before being put away in the pantry. She could hear voices coming from the kitchen and, after washing her hands, she went through and saw that Hettie had a visitor.

'Hello Gloria,' Thea greeted her with a welcoming smile.

'Hello, ducks.' Gloria beamed, her curved lips bright with red lipstick. 'You come to help with the Christmas party planning? Any good ideas are most welcome.'

'I'm not sure if I can think of anything to add.' Thea pulled out a chair opposite Hettie and sat down at the table. 'When is it?'

'In five weeks' time on the Saturday before Christmas as usual. So it's on the twentieth of December, this year,' Hettie said.

'Oh, that's the day Anna's coming home,' Thea said. 'She

told me in her last letter. I'm looking forward to having her here again for a while.'

It was always a pleasure to have Anna come and stay, Thea thought. The young woman had first arrived at Rookery House back in early spring last year and had quickly become part of their Rookery House family. Anna now spent most of her time away teaching at a school, but she came home in the holidays when she could.

'She can come along to the party,' Gloria said. 'It will be good to see her.'

Thea nodded. 'I'm sure she'd like that. It would be a chance for Anna to see lots of people from the village all together. So…' Thea glanced at the list written on the paper that lay on the table in front of Hettie. 'What have you got planned?'

'Lady Campbell-Gryce is donating a Christmas tree again and the Girl Guides will decorate it.' Hettie tapped each item on the list with her finger. 'Her Ladyship's loaning her gramophone player and some records to provide the music. The Mother's Day Club is making decorations. We've still got the ones from our previous parties, but the more we have, the better!' Hettie's eyes twinkled behind her round glasses. 'There'll be dancing, and games for the children. Everyone coming is bringing something to contribute to the food.'

'You're sure you've booked the village hall for the Christmas party?' Thea asked.

Hettie glanced briefly at Gloria, who gave a nod of her head, making her bottle-blonde, Pompadour hairstyle sway.

'We certainly 'ave,' Gloria's tone was firm. 'We ain't 'aving no one mess things up with the party again, not like 'appened with our first one! If Victor and his cronies want an emergency meeting, then Lady Campbell-Gryce 'as offered them a room at the Hall to use. But after the uproar caused by Victor throwing us out of the village 'all back in thirty-nine, I don't think he'd dare to try again, if 'e knows what's good for 'im.'

'Victor received a barrage of complaints from villagers for the way he behaved. Prue told me even Lady Campbell-Gryce sent him a note criticising his actions. She was most displeased at the way he'd ridden roughshod over the village's party arrangements,' Thea recalled. 'Victor might be a nasty piece of work, but he's no fool! I very much doubt there'll be any need for an emergency meeting on the day of the Christmas party this year.'

'I'm looking forward to it,' Hettie said. 'Our village Christmas party has become a popular occasion.'

'It gets everyone in the mood for Christmas,' Gloria added. 'We started it to make us feel better, didn't we, Hettie?' She put her arm around the older woman's shoulders, who was sitting next to her. 'And it snowballed from there. It made *everyone* feel better. We still need that while this war rumbles on.'

'We do. There's no sign of it ending any time soon,' Thea agreed. 'Taking joy from wherever we can is important. It keeps everyone going!'

Gloria let out a throaty laugh. 'Hark at us, we sound like sage old women!'

'Less of the old!' Hettie chuckled. 'But definitely sage! We have a great deal of wisdom between us, and we put it to good use, too.'

CHAPTER 22

Marianne walked as fast as she could towards Rookery House, pushing Emily along in the pram in front of her. The heavy grey clouds were threatening rain and she wanted to get back before it started to fall. She had been into the village to do some shopping, going to the butchers and Barker's grocers. It had taken far longer than she'd intended, what with having to wait in queues and seeing people she knew. Although, it had been nice to have a chat with friends – some of them fellow members of The Mother's Day Club, and other villagers who she'd got to know since she moved here.

She'd left the centre of the village and was walking fast along the lane that led to Rookery House, when she heard the ringing of a bicycle bell behind her. Steering the pram over towards the side of the road, she expected whoever was riding the bicycle to go past. Instead, the sound of the bell was replaced with the squeaking of brakes being applied.

Marianne looked around to see what was going on, just as the bicycle of the young lad who delivered telegrams in the village came to a stop alongside her.

'Mrs Fordham, from Rookery House?' he asked, not meeting her eyes.

'Yes, that's me,' she replied, the words feeling like dry cotton wool in her mouth, her heart beating faster. The arrival of a telegram boy these days was enough to put anyone on edge, and even more so if he was asking for you.

Marianne watched as he opened the bag slung around his shoulder and took out a buff-yellow envelope. The sight of it made her stomach sink as she immediately thought that something had happened to Alex.

He held it out to her. 'Telegram for you, Mrs Fordham.'

Marianne's first instinct was to tell him he could keep it. She did not want it. But telegrams didn't always bring bad news, she reminded herself. Perhaps Alex had some unexpected leave. But that was hardly likely so soon after their blissful time together last month, was it?

Reluctantly, Marianne took the envelope.

Relieved that his job was done, the telegram boy gave her a nod, mounted his bicycle again and quickly pedalled off back towards the village.

Left standing in the lane, she glanced at Emily, who thankfully was still asleep, having dropped off after they'd left the grocers. Wearing a white knitted hat that Hettie had made for her, the little girl was snug and warm, tucked under the blankets. Marianne was grateful that she was unaware of what was going on.

Turning her attention to the telegram in her gloved hand, she checked the name and address on the front. There was no mistake. It was for her. She swallowed hard, then slipping off her right glove, she ripped the envelope and took out the folded piece of thin paper, opened it and read the printed words.

REGRET TO INFORM YOU THAT YOUR
HUSBAND 69361 PILOT/OFFICER ALEX
FORDHAM IS REPORTED MISSING AS THE
RESULT OF AIR OPERATIONS ON 16 NOVEMBER
1941 STOP LETTER FOLLOWS STOP ANY
FURTHER INFORMATION RECEIVED WILL BE
IMMEDIATELY COMMUNICATED TO YOU STOP

Marianne gasped, putting a hand to her mouth. This couldn't be true. Alex mustn't be missing. He mustn't! Her eyes read through the words again, their meaning as sharp as if they were stabbing into her heart. She knew the air force would never have sent this unless it had really happened. Alex must have gone missing last night, just hours after she'd spoken to him. She frowned. It had been unlike him to telephone before an op. Had he known or sensed what was going to happen?

Tears stung Marianne's eyes. Where was he? What had happened to him? And… was he… she didn't want to think it, but was he gone? Was he dead?

Marianne could feel herself shaking and leaned against the handle of the pram, her tears falling as she stood all alone except for her sleeping daughter. Gasping as her sobs increased, she looked up at the grey sky, and felt cold splashes of rain land on her cheeks. It was as if the sky was crying alongside her.

As the raindrops became more frequent and heavier, Marianne shook her head and, with an enormous effort, pulled herself together. She needed to get Emily home. Beyond that, she couldn't think.

Stuffing the telegram into her coat pocket, Marianne somehow made her way back to Rookery House. It felt as if her world had suddenly shifted on its axis in the last few minutes since she'd read those dreadful words about Alex.

Leaving Emily sleeping safely in her pram, Marianne stumbled into the kitchen. The energy that had spurred her on to get home had drained away. Her appearance must have alerted Hettie because the older woman immediately abandoned whatever she was mixing up in the large brown, stoneware bowl and hurried towards Marianne.

'Whatever's the matter?' Hettie's face was full of concern. 'Is it the baby?'

Marianne shook her head, aware that her usual bouncy curls had become flattened against her face and neck from the rain. She delved into the pocket of her coat, pulled out the telegram and held it out.

Hettie's face drained of colour. 'Is it...?'

'Read it,' Marianne cut in and pulled out a chair and slumped down onto it, still wearing her damp coat. She was aware of the sharp intake of breath as her friend read the awful words on the telegram. Marianne hung her head, not wanting to believe what had happened, how her worries that something would happen to Alex had finally come true.

'Let's get you out of that wet coat,' Hettie said in a gentle voice.

Marianne stood up and allowed the older woman to help her off with her coat and then sat down again, while Hettie hung it over the back of a chair near the range to dry.

Returning to Marianne's side, Hettie took hold of both of Marianne's hands in hers. 'This is a terrible shock to you, but I want you to promise me that you won't give up hope that Alex is out there somewhere, alive. There is *always* hope.'

'But...' Marianne began.

113

'No buts! You need to focus on staying positive, keeping hopeful, not just for your sake but for Emily and this little one.' Hettie gestured towards Marianne's rounded belly. 'If you go getting yourself all worked up, it's not going to help you.' The older woman gently took hold of Marianne's chin and lifted it so that their gaze met. 'You understand?'

Marianne bit her bottom lip as tears flooded into her eyes. 'What shall I do if Alex is gone? If he doesn't ever come back?'

'Don't go crossing that bridge until you need to.' Hettie's tone was firm but kind. 'You're not alone. You have many people here who care for you and Emily. We'll do all we can to support you now and in the future.'

'Thank you.' Marianne's voice was hoarse as she battled to stop herself from dissolving into floods of tears. Hettie was right, thinking the worst was not going to help her. Marianne needed to think of Emily and her unborn child, but what if…? She squeezed her hands into fists, fighting back that thought. Taking a deep breath, she managed a watery smile. 'I'll do my best.'

'Good. Remember, we're all here for you.' Hettie's blue eyes were bright with unshed tears and she stepped closer and wrapped her arms around Marianne.

Sinking into her friend's warm embrace, Marianne sent up a silent prayer that Alex was alive out there somewhere and that he'd come back to her and their children. The thought that he wouldn't was just too unbearable.

CHAPTER 23

Evie had been tasked with changing the dressings of patients on Library Ward a short while ago at the morning briefing. Now she was on her way to the room in the old servants' area of the Hall, where they kept all the equipment and supplies for the job. Evie was not going alone. Matron had decided it was time for Delia to get some experience with dressings, but purely in an observational role and had given the young woman strict instructions to shadow Evie, watch carefully and learn.

'I was good at applying bandages on my first aid course,' Delia said, striding along the long corridor beside Evie. 'The instructor complimented me on my neat work. Although that was only on another trainee nurse, not a real patient with injuries.'

Evie gave her a sideways glance. 'That's a good start, although doing a dressing on proper injuries can be a bit more challenging, but once you get used to it, it's not so bad.'

They'd almost reached their destination when Evie saw a

familiar figure come in the back door, carrying a trug of freshly picked vegetables in each hand.

'Hello Ned,' Evie called.

He turned and looked their way and smiled. 'Evie! I was hoping to run into you. Have you got a minute?'

'Yes, do you need some help with those?' Evie gestured to the trugs.

'No, thanks. I've got something for you. Can you wait while I take these to Cook first?' he asked.

'Of course,' Evie replied.

'Who's that?' Delia's face was full of curiosity as Ned went into the kitchen.

'I'll tell you in a minute. Just wait here.' Evie pointed to a spot outside the door to the dressing supplies room. 'Don't go in without me. I won't be long.'

Leaving Delia, Evie hurried towards the kitchen and met Ned in the doorway as he was coming out. 'What did you want to give me?'

He removed a book from the pocket of his tweed jacket and held it out to her. 'I finished this last night, so now it's your turn to read it.'

Evie took the book and looked at the cover. It was Agatha Christie's latest Hercule Poirot novel which Ned had told her about after they'd had tea with Matron last week. 'Thank you. I look forward to reading it.' She gave him a grateful smile.

'What are you doing this morning?' Ned asked.

'I've got to change the patients' dressings on Library Ward and have come down here to prepare the equipment trolley first. Matron Reed ordered Delia to observe me.' She gave a nod of her head back over her shoulder towards where Delia was waiting further down the long corridor.

'You were very good at changing my dressing, as I recall,' Ned said. 'So gentle and kind.'

'Thank you, I'm pleased to hear that.' She gave him a smile of appreciation. 'I'd better go. Matron will be on patrol and wondering what's keeping me. Thanks for this.' She waved the book in the air as she hurried off to the nearby cloakroom, where she put it safely in her greatcoat pocket to take back to Rookery House with her later.

'Who was that?' Delia asked again as they went into the supply room and Evie started to gather what she needed.

'Ned Blythe. He used to be a patient here and he's a friend of mine,' Evie explained, putting a metal drum of sterilised dressings on the trolley.

'What's he doing here now?'

'He works in the garden.' Evie paused what she was doing. 'Forget the questions. What we need to focus on *now* is preparing this dressings trolley. If we leave something behind because of not concentrating on what we're supposed to be doing, it could cause problems for the patient. Even lead to potential infections. Understand?' Evie gave Delia a firm stare and the young woman nodded. 'Good. Now pass me that jar of disinfectant with the forceps in it, please?'

Back on Library Ward, Evie began changing Private Chambers' dressing where his right leg had been amputated.

'Before I remove the final layer of lint, I always double check everything is ready to apply the new dressing,' Evie explained to Delia, who stood beside her. 'Take a look at the trolley and see for yourself.'

Delia did as she was asked and gave Evie a nod.

'I'm going to remove the lint slowly and carefully with my sterile forceps.' Evie worked slowly, casting a quick glance at Private Chambers, who was staring up at the ceiling.

'Oh!' Delia exclaimed as his wound beneath the dressing was revealed.

Evie looked at her fellow nurse, who'd gone white; her eyes were wide and she was swaying slightly.

'Hazel!' Evie called to her friend, who had just wheeled a wicker basket of clean laundry into the ward ready to change the beds after all the dressings had been changed.

Hazel immediately saw what was happening, dashed over, grabbed hold of Delia and pushed her down onto the chair at the side of Private Chambers' bed, sitting with her back to Evie. 'You sit there and talk to our patient, Delia,' Hazel instructed. 'It often helps to talk while dressings are being changed and you're good at talking to patients.' She patted Delia's shoulder.

'Thank you,' Evie mouthed to Hazel, grateful that her friend had been on hand to assist, otherwise it was likely that Delia would have fainted and hit the floor.

'I'm glad to see you're not sitting on my bed this time,' Private Chambers said, turning his attention from the ceiling to Delia. 'It's fine for Nurse Hastings to sit on a chair next to my bed, isn't it Nurse Jones?'

'It is.' Evie gave the young soldier a smile. 'You're in luck today and have Nurse Hastings to talk to you while I change the dressing. Two nurses looking after you.'

'Tell me, Private Chambers,' Delia said, having recovered herself. 'Where did you live before you joined the army?'

Evie only half-listened to the conversation going on between Delia and her patient. Her attention was focused on checking the wound was healing well and then carefully applying a new sterile dressing. She'd almost finished when she heard the tapping of quick footsteps over the polished floor.

'*What is the meaning of this?*' Matron demanded, her voice controlled, but her displeasure evident. 'Nurse Hastings, you were told to observe Nurse Jones, not sit with a patient.'

'It's my fault, Matron,' Private Chambers said. 'I was feeling a bit bad with the dressing being changed and Nurse Hastings stepped in and distracted me, kept me calm so I could keep still for Nurse Jones.' He gave Matron a smile. 'Honestly, she helped me and without her distraction...' He held up both his plastered arms in questioning gesture. 'Please don't be cross with her.'

'Very well, I'm glad she could help you,' Matron conceded. 'Good nursing is about judging what a patient needs and when.'

'Matron Reed, there you are!' Lady Campbell-Gryce came hurrying into the ward, a notebook and pen in her hand.

As Matron turned her attention to her Ladyship, Evie caught Private Chambers' eye and he winked at her. She gave him a grateful smile, relieved that his quick thinking had saved Delia and probably herself from a ticking off by Matron.

'Can we talk about the arrangements for Christmas?' Lady Campbell-Gryce asked. 'I'm not sure if there's anything different that you'd like to do this year.'

'Yes certainly,' Matron agreed. 'I'll be with you in a moment.' She turned back to them. 'When you've finished the dressings, Nurses Jones and Hastings, you can help Nurse Robertson change the beds.' With a nod, she headed off to discuss Christmas.

'That was close!' Hazel breathed out a sigh of relief. 'You saved us from a spot of bother there, Private Chambers.'

He grinned. 'My pleasure, and it was lovely to talk to you, Nurse Hastings. You really did help distract me.'

'Thank you so much. I must admit I don't think I'm very good at changing the dressings on real injuries. It's a lot different to practising on another trainee. But...' Delia beamed. 'I can talk wonderfully well, can't I?'

Evie caught Hazel's eye and they both started to laugh and Private Chambers and Delia joined in too.

CHAPTER 24

The last time Marianne had walked along this lane, her world had been so different. As far as she'd been aware, her husband was safe and well. Was that just yesterday, less than twenty-four hours ago? Marianne thought as she pushed the pram in front of her. Somehow it felt so much longer. The many hours of the night that she'd lain awake had seemed stretched and distorted in time. Since the telegram boy had delivered that awful news, Marianne's world had shifted, and she didn't want to accept this new reality.

'Look!' Emily, who was sitting up in the pram, pointed to the flock of rooks flying overhead, wheeling on the gusts of wind. Rising and falling, tumbling, twisting and climbing, they looked as if they were playing on the air currents.

Marianne smiled at her daughter, who was blissfully unaware of what had happened to her father, and Marianne was determined that Emily should remain that way for the time being. 'The rooks are enjoying flying in the wind.'

Emily laughed and stretched out her arms, flapping them like a bird.

They were heading into the village to this morning's Mother's Day Club. Marianne wanted to go as usual in a bid to keep things as normal as possible for both Emily and her. Nothing could erase the awful hollow feeling that had settled in the pit of Marianne's stomach after hearing that Alex was Missing In Action, but at least by keeping occupied she could perhaps distract herself for a short while.

Everyone at Rookery House had been so kind and understanding, showering them both with love and support, and she was grateful to have such warm and loving people around her. Hettie's firm voice of reason yesterday had prevented Marianne from plunging into the depths of despair. Although it hadn't stopped her from lying awake most of the night, leaving her feeling wrung out and exhausted this morning. But at least if she was tired now, perhaps she would sleep better tonight.

Arriving at the village hall, she parked the pram alongside other prams and pushchairs then unclipped Emily's safety harness and lifted her out. Holding on to her daughter's hand, they walked into the hall and were greeted by the sound of chatter from the mothers and children who'd already arrived. After taking off Emily's hat and coat, and Marianne's own outer garments, they headed over to the children's corner.

Without needing any encouragement, Emily joined the other children and was soon absorbed in playing with the much-loved tea set with two other little girls. Marianne stood and watched them for a few moments, smiling at how they mimicked what they saw adults doing.

'Marianne,' a familiar voice called.

She turned around and saw Gloria and her daughter Dora heading towards them, having just arrived. Like Emily, Dora quickly joined in with the others, playing with the tea set.

'Hello.' Marianne gave her friend a smile.

'I've finished my dress. What you think?' Gloria asked, putting one hand on her hip. 'I think Sylvia's old curtains look better on me. Making a pattern from an old dress 'as worked brilliantly!'

Marianne cast her eyes over Gloria's dress. It fitted perfectly and emphasised her curvy figure. 'It looks wonderful. You've done an excellent job.'

Gloria beamed at her, her pink lipsticked lips matching the shade of the flowers on her dress. 'Thank you. I'm delighted with 'ow it's turned out and I'll be making more of them. You've taught us so well and I'm very grateful.'

Marianne's eyes suddenly filled with tears at her friend's kind words and she had to bite her bottom lip to stop it trembling as a wave of emotion flooded through her.

Gloria's face was full of concern. 'Let's get you out of here for a minute.' She turned to one of the mothers who was supervising the children's corner. 'We'll be in the kitchen if you need us.' Then Gloria took hold of Marianne's elbow and guided her across the hall and through the door leading into the kitchen, closing it behind them.

'What's the matter?' Gloria asked in a kind voice. 'Has anything happened?'

Marianne nodded, and as she did so, her tears spilled over and ran down her cheeks. 'Alex is Missing In Action. I had a telegram yesterday.'

Without saying a word, Gloria stepped towards Marianne and enveloped her in a tight perfumy embrace.

Gloria's action unleashed Marianne's sobs and she cried into her friend's shoulder. When her sobs finally subsided, she took a step back. 'I'm sorry, I've made your beautiful dress wet.' She gestured at the damp patch on Gloria's shoulder.

'Don't you worry about that, ducks,' Gloria reassured her. 'It will dry. I'm so sorry to 'ear that, do you know what 'appened?'

Marianne shook her head. 'No, not yet. But I've been imagining different scenarios. I'm trying not to. Hettie told me not to cross any bridges until I have to. But it's hard not to think the worst that…' Her voice wavered and she covered her face with her hands for a few moments.

'It's easier to say than do, ain't it?' Gloria said in a sympathetic tone. 'All you can do is wait and hope.'

Marianne nodded. 'I'm trying. I want to keep things normal for Emily. That's why I came here this morning.'

'It's better for you to be here too, rather than sitting at home worrying. I ain't saying that you shouldn't be worrying because I know I would be in your shoes. We do it anyway, don't we? At least being 'ere we can keep you busy and keep you company.' Gloria put her arm around Marianne's shoulders. 'Splash some water on your face and then why don't we go and tackle some of that mendin' that needs to be done? Prue's managed to get 'old of some more children's clothes for the clothing depot, but some of the garments need repairing and your sewing expertise would be appreciated.'

Marianne managed a watery smile and nodded. 'I'd rather be busy and sewing always soothes me.'

'That's the way, ducks.' Gloria squeezed Marianne's shoulders before letting her go. 'Keep your chin up. You're not alone with this, we are all 'ere for you. I'll see you in the 'all in a minute, all right?'

'Thank you,' Marianne said gratefully.

Left alone in the kitchen, she splashed her face with cold water at the sink and took a few moments to gather herself together. She was grateful for Gloria's support and understanding and knew that out there in the hall the other women would be the same. Spending time with them was always like wrapping herself in a soft and warmly comforting blanket. Right now, Marianne needed that more than ever.

CHAPTER 25

Marianne had just closed the door of the bedroom she shared with Emily, having put her daughter down for a nap, when she heard the rattle of the letter box with the arrival of the afternoon post. Instantly, her thoughts jumped to possible news of Alex. It was just over two weeks since he'd gone missing and November had made way for December, but Marianne still didn't know what had happened to her husband. In those long days and even longer nights, she had done her best to remain hopeful that he was out there somewhere alive and that he would come back to them safely.

She made her way down the stairs and along to the front door, where three letters lay on the mat. Could any of them be for her? Carefully crouching down, taking care as her belly had grown even larger in the past few weeks, with the baby due to be born later in the month, Marianne scooped up the envelopes and took hold of the door handle to steady herself as she stood up. Turning them over, she saw that there was a letter for Thea, one for Flo and the last was for her. Staring at her name and address, she didn't recognise the spiky handwriting, but the postmark made her gasp. It was the same as had always been franked on the letters that Alex had sent her from his aerodrome in Lincolnshire.

Heading through to the kitchen, Marianne was grateful that she was alone in the house. Hettie and Thea had gone into Wykeham as it was market day, while Flo was outside working with Alice. Marianne put the letters for the others on a dresser and then took hers over to the table, pulled out a chair and sat down. She took a deep breath, opened the envelope and removed a folded, single sheet of paper. Opening it, her eyes dropped to the signature at the bottom. It said *Henry Smith (Smithy)*. Marianne recognised the name. Alex had talked about his friend Smithy when they were last together. It had been Smithy who had loaned Alex his red sports car to come and visit her. Marianne's eyes quickly went to the top of the letter and she began to read.

Dear Marianne,

You will have been informed that Alex is Missing In Action and I expect are desperate for word of him. Myself and others at the aerodrome are also anxious to hear what has become of our good friend. I have waited until now to write to contact you, in the hope that we would have had some news, but sadly, there has been nothing. Alex asked me, if anything should happen to him, to promise that I would write to you and tell you what I could about what happened because he felt not knowing would be hard for you to bear.
We were on an op over Germany and encountered heavy flak. I was flying behind Alex and saw that his plane was hit in one engine and it was losing height. I didn't see any parachutes before I lost sight of it. That doesn't mean there

weren't any or that Alex didn't manage to bring his plane down safely. I dearly hope that he and his crew bailed out or landed. More than that, I cannot say with any certainty. I hope that we will soon hear good news of Alex as he is greatly missed by all of us here. If I have any more information, I'll let you know.

With my regards,

Henry Smith (Smithy)

Marianne put a hand to her mouth. The idea that Alex's plane had been struck by enemy fire had, of course, gone through her mind so many times, but to read the words that it had been, hit her hard like a punch to the stomach. What had happened to him and his crew? Had they bailed out? Being the pilot, Alex would be the last to go, and she knew that he would always have put his crewmates first. He would do all he could to save them, even if he couldn't save himself. But if they had all bailed out, what then? They would have landed on enemy territory…

The letter had provided her with some answers, but it had given rise to even more questions, more unknowns. Marianne let out a sigh, her heart heavy with worry at the thought of what Alex had gone through in those moments after his plane had been hit. Had he survived? Or was she a widow and Emily fatherless, but they just didn't know it yet?

CHAPTER 26

Thea put some hay and leaves from a winter cabbage into the run for the doe rabbit, Flopsy, then carefully secured the catch onto the wooden hutch. She'd just cleaned out both rabbit's hutches and fed them, a job George always helped with when he wasn't at school.

Crouching down, Thea watched Flopsy eating, the brown and white rabbit's nose and whiskers twitching as she munched contentedly on a cabbage leaf.

Having rabbits at Rookery House had been a great success, Thea thought, standing up. Flopsy had given birth to two litters this year and was now having the winter to rest before she'd hopefully have more babies next year. The young rabbits had grown fast, fed on the plentiful supply of plants which Flo and George had foraged for them around the hedgerows. The last of the second litter had gone a few weeks ago, leaving just Flopsy and Benjamin here. It had been hard to see the young rabbits go, but right from the start it had been the plan and the whole point of keeping them was to help supplement meat supplies.

'Auntie Thea,' a child's voice called.

Thea turned around to see Emily running towards her in her slow toddling way, a beaming smile on her face under her woollen hat. She was dressed warmly in a coat and mittens. Walking just behind was Marianne.

Thea reached down and scooped the little girl up into her arms. 'Have you come to see the rabbits?'

Emily nodded and wriggled to be put down. After Thea released her, the little girl crouched down next to Flopsy's run to watch the rabbit eat, as she often did with George.

'I thought you were going to The Mother's Day Club this morning,' Thea said to Marianne, who'd come to stand beside her, watching as her daughter poked a blade of grass she'd plucked in through the wire of the run for Flopsy.

'I changed my mind as I didn't feel up to it,' Marianne said in a flat voice.

Thea studied the young woman's face, noticing that she looked tired and pale. 'Are you feeling unwell?'

'No, I'm fine. I've been helping Hettie make the butter.' She gave a heavy sigh. 'It's just my mind's on other things this morning…' She halted as her eyes filled with tears.

Thea put her arm around Marianne. 'Has something happened?'

Marianne nodded. 'I had a letter from Smithy yesterday. He's one of Alex's friends and another pilot. He loaned Alex the red sports car to take us on our little holiday on his last leave.' She took a deep breath before continuing in a hushed voice, 'Smithy wrote that he was flying behind Alex and saw that his plane was hit and was going down. He didn't see any parachutes before he lost sight of it…' Tears rolled down Marianne's face and she dashed them away with her gloved hand. 'Alex asked Smithy to write to me if anything happened to him. He wanted me to know the facts. But I still have no idea if Alex is alive… or not.'

Thea wrapped her arms around Marianne. She wished there was some way she could ease her friend's pain and torment. Having Alex proclaimed Missing In Action was so full of uncertainty. It gave Marianne hope and yet prolonged her suffering and anxiety over her husband's fate, which wasn't good for an expectant mother.

'Does Smithy think Alex managed to land the plane?' Thea asked, stepping back and looking at Marianne, whose face was streaked with tears.

'He didn't say. His letter told me what he saw but has left me with even more questions that I can't answer.' Marianne glanced up at the grey sky. 'Is he still out there somewhere? Will he come home to us, or not? If he doesn't, then what will become of us? What will we do?'

'Mamma.' Emily stared up at her mother, her face anxious, clearly picking up on Marianne's distress.

'It's all right, darling,' Marianne reassured her daughter with a smile. 'Can you pick some more grass to feed Flopsy with?'

Emily nodded and plucked some more blades and returned her attention to the rabbit.

'If the worst happens, and I hope with all my heart it doesn't, you will *always* have a home here with me for as long as you want.' Thea kept her voice low. 'You are part of the Rookery House family, Marianne. You, Emily and this little one.' Thea nodded towards Marianne's belly, which her green winter coat didn't cover now, only the buttons at the top doing up.

Marianne managed a weak smile. 'Thank you, I appreciate that.'

'Whatever happens in the future, we are all here for you and will help you through,' Thea reassured her.

She hoped that Alex was one of the lucky ones and had survived his plane going down. But if Thea was honest with herself, the stark reality was that many young men were being killed each day as they flew ops over enemy territory. Alex could so easily be one of them. Still, until they knew for sure what had happened to him, Thea would keep hoping that Marianne would be reunited with her husband.

CHAPTER 27

Evie wound her soft, blue wool scarf around her neck and then put on her heavy greatcoat, knowing that the cold temperature outside would be a sharp contrast to the warmth of the kitchen here at Rookery House.

'You need to wrap up well out there today,' Hettie said. 'That wind's straight from the North Pole and goes right through you. But I suppose we should expect that in December!'

'I'll soon warm up once I start bicycling.' Evie put on her blue knitted beret which matched her scarf, tucking in some loose strands of her auburn hair. Then she pulled on her gloves to complete her outfit, ready to face the elements.

This Saturday afternoon she was going to be cycling into Wykeham with Ned. They planned to have a look around, go to the book shop and then to a tea shop. It would be the first time they'd had the chance to spend any length of time together to have a long talk. All their chats since Ned had arrived to work at the Hall had been snatched in odd moments when they happened to meet at the hospital. They'd all been brief as one or both of them had been on their way to do one job or another or else had to rush off somewhere carrying out orders. Evie was looking forward to having a proper conversation with Ned, an opportunity to discuss the two books he'd loaned her to read and whatever else they drifted into.

'If you want to invite Ned to come and have his tea here later, he'd be most welcome. I'm making an oxtail and vegetable soup.' Hettie gestured to the pile of vegetables that she was cutting up, sat at the table. 'There'll be fresh baked bread to go with it and apple pie and custard for afters. Food to warm and fill us up is what's needed today.'

'Thank you, Hettie. I'm not sure if Ned's expected at the Whites for his tea. I can ask him.'

'I hope you'll have a lovely time this afternoon. You work hard and deserve some fun,' Hettie said.

'Thank you, I'm sure I will.' Evie picked up her bag. 'I'll see you later.' She went out of the back door and headed to the shed where she kept her bicycle. Then she pushed it round to the front gate to wait for Ned, who was cycling here from the head gardener's cottage on Great Plumstead Hall estate where he lived.

As she waited, Evie thought Hettie was right about the wind. It did indeed seem to go through her, icy blasts finding their way in through any gaps in her clothing and chilling her skin.

The sight of Ned pedalling around the corner towards her was a welcome one, and rather than waiting for him to stop, Evie mounted her bicycle, ready to leave as soon as he drew level.

'Hello, I'm cold, so need to get moving,' she said as he reached her.

'It's not so bad once you start pedalling,' Ned replied, riding along beside her.

Within a few minutes, as they passed through the centre of Great Plumstead, taking the road that led to Wykeham, Evie was already feeling warmer.

They made good time, only having to stop once, pulling over in a gateway while two lorries lumbered past, heading in the direction of the aerodrome.

'I was talking to Lady Campbell-Gryce's housekeeper Ada the other day,' Ned said. 'She told me about having to move out of her cottage to make way for the aerodrome.'

'That's right. She's Hettie's sister and came to live at Rookery House for a while before she got the job as housekeeper. It was very upsetting for Ada. She'd lived in that house for a long time,' Evie explained as they set off again, riding side by side.

'It's caused a lot of disruption around here by the sound of it. When's it due to open?' Ned asked.

'In the spring, I think. As soon as it's ready, I suppose,' Evie replied. 'Then it will bring a whole different sort of disruption with an influx of airmen and noisy planes taking off.'

'That's war for you. It disrupts and destroys in so many ways.' Ned shook his head. 'Let's not talk about the war any more. We're supposed to be having a lovely afternoon.'

Evie glanced across at him. 'I agree. We'll just discuss books and things that make us happy. Agreed?'

'Agreed,' Ned confirmed in a serious tone, before giving a laugh.

❧

Arriving in Wykeham, they parked their bicycles and started with a wander around looking in the windows of the various shops surrounding the market square. Then they meandered up side streets before heading for their ultimate destination of the book shop.

'Ah Mr Blythe, I have a book waiting for you,' the owner greeted them as they stepped inside the shop, the bell jangling overhead.

'I've ordered the new A. J. Cronin novel, *The Keys to the Kingdom*,' Ned said, turning briefly to Evie, before approaching the wooden counter where the shop owner had taken the book out from behind it and laid it reverently on top.

Ned picked it up, then took a good look at the cover, front and back, before opening it at the start and beginning to read.

The owner caught Evie's eye and gave her a smile, clearly understanding Ned's appreciation of a shiny new book.

Evie returned the older man's smile, knowing that Ned was especially fond of A. J. Cronin's books and had encouraged her to read some of his work, which she'd enjoyed.

'It's a beauty.' Ned closed the book after a few moments. 'I'm going to enjoy this. How much do I owe you?'

While Ned settled his bill for the book, Evie drifted off and wandered around the shop, stopping now and then when her attention was caught by a title she'd not read before.

'I've had a load of new second-hand stock in that I haven't had time to put out yet,' the owner called over to her, pointing to a box of books on a chair by the counter.

Unable to resist, Evie went over to look. She gasped as her eyes fell on Jane Austen's *Persuasion*. She'd read it before, borrowed from a library, with the intention of buying her own copy one day, but somehow hadn't… until now. Taking it from the box, she saw it was in excellent condition and she decided to buy it to add to her much-loved book collection.

By the time they left the shop a short while later, Ned had added another two books from the second-hand box to his purchases as well.

'Time for some tea?' Evie asked.

'Definitely,' Ned agreed.

Once they were seated by the bay window of the little tea shop that overlooked the market square, a pot of tea and a scone each in front of them, Evie took out the copy of *Persuasion* from her bag.

'It's in beautiful condition. It hardly looks like it has been read.' She stroked the cover and then flicked through the pages. 'I don't know why anyone would get rid of it.'

'Not everyone feels the same way about books as we do,' Ned said, pouring out cups of tea.

Evie grinned. 'I know, still it's my gain that whoever bought it new didn't want to keep it. But I will! It's now part of my book collection and shall stay with me forever. Though you can borrow it if you'd like to.'

'Thank you, I haven't read it and *would* like to.' Ned added milk to his tea from the little jug and stirred it in. 'We didn't have many books in the house when I was growing up, apart from the Bible and father's gardening reference ones. It makes me appreciate being able to buy them for myself now.'

'How did you become such an avid reader, then?' Evie asked, spreading some jam on her scone.

'I borrowed books from the nearest library. It was only a little one, but it instilled a love of reading in me. I read everything they had several times over.'

'I was fortunate,' said Evie. 'My father was a great reader, and we had a *lot* of books. Mother even gave me some of my father's books when I got married and left home.' She fell silent for a moment, picturing those precious books, and the others that she had added to her collection, carefully arranged in the bookcase in the bedroom she'd shared with Douglas in their flat in London. Her late husband had refused to let her have her books in the sitting room, declaring they would spoil the decor. Not being a reader, Douglas had had no appreciation of their value. In hindsight, that had been a good thing, Evie thought. He'd had no idea what a treasured escape reading had given her, otherwise he would have stopped her from reading just as he'd done with other things he didn't approve of.

'Evie?' Ned's voice broke into her thoughts. 'Are you all right?'

She looked at him and managed a smile. 'I'm fine. A memory came back to me, that's all.'

Ned's face looked concerned. 'Not a good one from how pale you've gone. Are you sure you're all right?'

'Yes, honestly. I was just thinking about my books and how they helped me escape during the dark days of my marriage. When I left London, I had to leave them behind to make it look like I'd been…' she lowered her voice to a whisper, '*killed in the Blitz*. That was hard to do, so I'm grateful I was able to return and get them after you found out Douglas was gone for ever and I was safe. Now when I read them, I'm not doing so to escape my awful marriage, but simply to relax and enjoy the story.' She leaned back in her chair and gave him a warm smile. 'They feel different to read now, just as lovely, but I'm no longer reading with one ear cocked listening for Douglas to come home.'

'I'm glad you could retrieve your books,' Ned said, his grey eyes full of understanding. 'They've been with you through the ups and downs. They are part of your experience.'

Evie nodded. 'That's right. Now, tell me what you thought

of *For Whom the Bell Tolls,* and then I'll tell you what I think? After that we can talk about the latest Hercule Poirot book.'

Heading back to Great Plumstead, bicycling along side by side with the brisk north wind on their backs, Evie was delighted with the afternoon they'd spent together. After a long discussion about books in the tea shop, their conversation had drifted on to other topics, the pair of them never being short of things to say to each other. She wasn't ready to end their time together yet.

'Hettie said I could invite you to have tea with us at Rookery House. Would you like to come? Hettie's a marvellous cook and there's oxtail and vegetable soup on the menu, followed by apple pie and custard,' Evie asked as she pedalled steadily along.

Ned glanced across at her, looking surprised but then pleased at the invitation. 'That would be lovely, thank you.'

They pedalled faster and were soon at Rookery House. When they went into the warm kitchen it was filled with the delicious aroma of the hearty soup simmering on the range and the freshly baked bread cooling on a rack on the table.

'That smells so good, Hettie,' Evie said to the older woman who was putting the finishing touches to the pastry decoration on top of the apple pie. 'I've brought Ned home for tea like you said. Ned, this is Hettie, Hettie, meet Ned.'

Hettie gave him a warm, beaming smile. 'It's good to meet you, lad. I've heard lots about you from Evie. Welcome to Rookery House.'

'Thank you. I'm pleased to meet you,' Ned said. 'Thank you for inviting me to tea. It's very kind of you.'

'You're very welcome. I always make plenty to go round.

So how did you get on in Wykeham? Did you buy any books?' Hettie asked.

Evie and Ned looked at each other and burst into laughter.

'You could say that!' Evie held up her bag. 'I found a lovely second-hand copy of *Persuasion* and Ned bought a few books, too. We'll be swapping them around so we can both read them.'

At that moment, the door from the hall burst open and George came rushing in with some books in his hands. 'Will you…?' he began, but halted as he spotted Ned.

'Will we what?' Hettie prompted him.

George cast an uncertain glance at Ned before going over to Hettie. 'Can you read to me, please?'

'I can't for a bit my lovely. I've got to finish this for our tea and my hands are covered in flour.' Hettie held up her floury hands for him to see.

George looked disappointed. Evie knew how much the little boy loved his books and especially the Beatrix Potter ones clutched in his hands.

'How about I read them to you?' Evie glanced at Ned, who smiled at her. 'We'll just take our coats off first.'

'Thank you.' George beamed at her, pulled out a chair at the table and sat down, ready.

'Shall we take it in turns to read a page each?' Ned suggested as they both took a seat at the table, one on each side of George.

Evie looked at him in astonishment. 'You want to read too? It's different from what you usually read.'

'Of course, but I'm sure it's a good story, isn't it George?' Ned asked.

The little boy nodded, his face serious.

'I enjoy an entertaining story, whatever age it's written for,' Ned explained.

'In that case,' Evie said, opening *The Tale of Benjamin Bunny* and turning to the first page, laying the book in front of George so they could all see it, 'we'll take it in turns to do a page. George, you can turn the pages for us. Shall I go first?'

Ned looked at her over the top of George's head and grinned, his eyes twinkling behind his glasses. 'I'm ready when you are.'

Evie gave him a nod and began to read, 'One morning…'

The kitchen was quiet. Ned had gone home, Thea and Marianne had taken the children up to get ready for bed, and Flo had gone out to do a final check of the animals. It was just Evie and Hettie putting the last of the cleaned crockery away from their meal.

'Thank you for inviting Ned,' Evie said, putting some plates and bowls back on one of the dressers. 'I think he enjoyed himself and he certainly loved your cooking.'

'Ned's most welcome any time. I liked him a lot. He's a lovely young man, Evie,' Hettie said.

The older woman's words made Evie halt what she was doing. She'd heard similar words before, only said about another man. Her mother had said the same about Douglas when she'd first met him, but how wrong she'd been!

'Evie, what do you think?' Hettie's voice brought Evie's attention back to the present.

'Sorry, I was miles away. What did you say?'

'I said it was lovely how Ned joined in reading to little George. Not many men would have the patience to do that,' Hettie said.

'Yes.' Evie forced a smile. 'Ned loves reading any books.'

It was true that Ned had shown great patience and care

over reading to George, not minding when they read the same book twice. It was something that Douglas would never have done. But then he wouldn't have even read it once to the little boy.

Hettie's words, which were so like her mother's, had unsettled Evie. They had stirred up bad memories and sadly tainted what had otherwise been a lovely afternoon and evening in Ned's company.

The memory of the past made her doubt her judgement. She'd been terribly wrong about Douglas. Perhaps she was a poor judge of how men really were. Although why was she so bothered about it? a voice in her head pointed out. Ned was only a friend after all, not her husband. If he ever turned out to be like Douglas she wasn't legally bound to him like she had been to her husband. So why had Hettie's comment upset her so much? Evie wondered. Did she feel more for Ned than she was prepared to admit to herself?

CHAPTER 28

Thea always enjoyed Sunday evenings. They were a time to relax and prepare for another busy week ahead. Tonight, with the rain splattering against the windows, sitting beside a warm fire with soothing music playing on the wireless felt even more enjoyable.

It had been a lovely day, she thought, watching the orange and gold flames flickering and the embers of the wood glow. She and Flo had taken the children for a walk in the woods before the weather changed. They'd returned to a delicious dinner of home-produced roast pork, apple sauce and piles of Rookery House grown vegetables. Then the afternoon had been spent playing games and reading as the rain had set in.

Now the children were tucked up in bed and fast asleep. Marianne had gone up for an early night, so it was just Thea and Hettie sitting by the fire, while Flo and Evie were playing a game of cards at the little table nearby.

'You're looking very thoughtful,' Hettie's voice cut into Thea's thoughts.

Thea turned her gaze to her friend who was watching her

while she knitted, her fingers seeming to fly as they worked on the sock she was knitting.

'I was just thinking what a lovely day it's been.'

'It has,' Hettie agreed. 'Are you out in the WVS canteen tomorrow?'

'Yes, and probably on Friday as well this week. Prue and I need to cover an extra shift. It's not so bad this time of year when things are a bit quieter in the garden here. I…' Thea halted at the sound of Big Ben's chimes coming over the wireless. She glanced at the clock on the mantlepiece. It was nine o'clock and time for the news.

'I'll just listen to what's been happening and then I'll get ready for bed,' Hettie said. 'I'm on duty at The Mother's Day Club in the morning.'

'*This is the BBC Home Service, and this is the news and this is Alvar Lidell reading it…*'

Thea listened in horror as the newsreader reported that Japan had carried out air attacks on American naval bases in the Pacific and that it had issued a formal declaration of war against the United States and Britain.

Hettie gasped, dropping her knitting in her lap and putting a hand to her mouth. Flo and Evie abandoned their game and hurried over to perch on the arms of Thea's and Hettie's armchairs. Evie, who was sitting by Hettie, put her arm around the older woman's shoulders.

They listened in silence, all with shocked and horrified expressions on their faces, as the newsreader went on to describe President Roosevelt's statement about how the American naval base on Hawaii had been attacked from the air. Manila in the Philippines had also been attacked. President Roosevelt had responded by mobilising the United States Army. As the newsreader described the air assault in more detail, it conjured up images in Thea's mind of smoke and destruction coming out of the blue, like she had experienced when she'd been in London at the start of the Blitz.

As the news came to an end, Thea got up and switched the wireless off, aware of the sharp change in the atmosphere in the room. Just a few minutes ago, they'd all been enjoying a relaxing Sunday evening, but that had been shattered by this latest news.

'What will happen now?' Flo asked, her face pale.

'Unless the Japanese stop attacking and change their mind about going to war with America, then I expect President Roosevelt will have no option but to declare war on Japan,' Thea said, in a heartfelt tone. 'I doubt Japan will back down so America will go to war.'

'The longer this war goes on, the worse it gets!' Hettie's voice was hoarse, her blue eyes bright with tears behind her round glasses. 'It's spreading all over the world.'

'What about Germany? Will the Americans join us in fighting the Nazis?' Evie asked.

'They will if Hitler declares war against America,' Thea said. 'Then he'll have the might of the Americans against him, and they are a much bigger country than us. We could do with them joining forces with us like they did in the Great War. We'll just have to wait and find out what happens over the next few days.' Thea looked around at her dear friends, sad to see the looks of distress on their faces at this latest news. 'There's nothing any of us can do to change it. We just need to keep on doing what we're doing. Like all the other women in the village.'

Hettie sniffed back her tears. 'You're right. What we do adds up and matters. If the women of Britain weren't pulling together and doing their bit for the war effort, then this country would be a lot worse off. Mind you, I think if it were women who ran countries, we wouldn't have got into a war in the first place! We have more sense!'

'I think you're right, Hettie,' Evie agreed. 'Maybe one day women will get the chance to lead countries. Imagine that. We could have a woman prime minister!'

Thea smiled at Evie, grateful to her for lightening the mood a little. The fact remained that the next few days could see a significant turning point in the war if America joined in with the Allies. All they could do was watch and wait.

CHAPTER 29

Marianne carefully hand-stitched around a buttonhole of the cream silk and lace blouse which she was making for Lady Campbell-Gryce. Hopefully, this morning she would be able to finish it as it was her last piece of commissioned sewing before the baby was born.

'For you.' Emily, who was sitting on the rug in front of the sitting room fireplace, held up a toy teacup to Marianne.

Marianne took the cup and pretended to take a sip. 'Thank you, that's just what I needed.' She gave her daughter an appreciative smile, glad that Emily was unaware of the turmoil and uncertainty that weighed heavily on her mother. Just over a week had passed since she'd received the letter from Smithy, but there was still no news about what had happened to Alex.

'More?' Emily asked.

Marianne nodded and held out the small teacup for the little girl to pretend to fill from her toy teapot. 'Thank you. Do you think Teddy and Polly need another cup too?'

Emily turned her attention to her much-loved teddy bear

and rag doll, whom she'd seated on the rug by the tea set and who were taking part in the imaginary tea party.

With her daughter happily occupied, chattering away to her toys using the words she had learned so far and some of her own making, Marianne returned to her sewing, listening to the sound of *Music While You Work* on the wireless. Once she'd finished the blouse, she would arrange a time to visit Lady Campbell-Gryce for a final fitting, then after that she needed to focus her efforts on preparing for the arrival of her new baby.

As if the baby knew Marianne was thinking about it, she felt a sharp prod of a knee or elbow on the inside of her belly. She rubbed her tummy over the spot, smiling to herself at the prospect of meeting this little one soon. Perhaps by the time it was born there'd be news of Alex... Maybe he'd even have returned, she thought hopefully.

A loud, sharp knocking on the front door of Rookery House startled Marianne. It was most unusual for anyone to knock on there, as most visitors went around the back of the house to the kitchen door. Whoever it was must be a stranger. Could it be someone with news of Alex?

She put her sewing to the side and stood up. 'Come on, Emily, let's go and answer the door.' She held out her hand to the little girl, who looked reluctant to leave her game. But before the pair of them could reach the door into the hall, it opened and Hettie popped her head around it.

'I'll go and see who it is,' she told them before closing it again.

Emily dashed back to her tea party on the rug and was soon engrossed in her make-believe game once more. Marianne stood waiting, unable to settle to her sewing again without knowing who was calling and why. She could hear voices but couldn't make out what they were saying. Then came the sound of the front door closing, followed by footsteps coming down the hall.

'Wait there a moment, please,' she heard Hettie say, moments before the sitting-room door opened and she stepped in, closing the door behind her.

'You've got a visitor,' Hettie said in a hushed voice. 'It's *Alex's mother*!'

Marianne gasped and grabbed the back of an armchair, her legs suddenly going soft as if the bones had dissolved inside them.

'Let's get you sitting down.' Hettie's face was full of concern as she took Marianne's arm and steered her back to where she'd been sewing a few moments ago.

'I've never met her before,' Marianne whispered, as she sat down in the armchair. 'What does she want? Has she got news about Alex?'

'She wouldn't tell me, just insisted on speaking to you. You don't have to see her if you'd rather not. I can send her away.' Hettie put a hand on Marianne's shoulder.

'She might have heard something, so I must talk to her. Will you ask her to come in, please?'

Hettie nodded and squeezed Marianne's shoulder gently before heading for the door.

Marianne braced herself. If she wasn't so desperate for any possible news of her husband, she would have refused to meet her mother-in-law for the first time without Alex by her side. Alex's mother had not approved of her son marrying someone she considered beneath him and hadn't attended their wedding. Since then Marianne knew that her husband had kept in contact with his parents and occasionally seen them on his own. However, they had shown no interest in meeting either her or Emily until now.

Hettie came into the room first and stood to the side as a

tall, haughty-looking figure swept in, a cloud of perfume emanating from her.

Marianne stood up and held out her hand. 'Hello.'

Mrs Fordham senior looked down her long nose at Marianne, ignoring her outstretched hand. 'I've come to speak with you.' Her eyes then fell briefly on Emily, who was staring up at her. 'I presume this is my son's daughter.'

'That's Emily. *Marianne* and Alex's lovely little girl,' Hettie said, her tone neutral despite the spark of annoyance flaring in her eyes behind her round glasses.

'Could you take the child somewhere else while we talk?' Mrs Fordham directed her question to Hettie.

'Is that all right with you, Marianne?' Hettie asked. 'Emily could come into the kitchen with me and I'll read her a story.'

Marianne had only been in the presence of her mother-in-law for a matter of moments, but she knew she disliked her. Instinct told her that it was best for Emily to go with Hettie, as her own flesh and blood grandmother was showing no indication of any pleasure at meeting her granddaughter for the first time. Mrs Fordham referring to Emily as *the child* spoke volumes.

'Yes, thank you. You go with Hettie, Emily. I just need to talk to this lady for a few minutes,' Marianne explained.

'Come on, my lovely.' Hettie held out her hand to the little girl, who willingly stood up and took hold of it, grabbing her teddy in her other hand, before casting a wary eye over her grandmother as she left the room.

As soon as the door closed behind them, Mrs Fordham sat down on the armchair opposite Marianne.

'Have you heard any news about Alex?' Marianne asked, sitting down again.

'No, and despite my husband making enquiries at the War Office, we know no more than Alex is still officially Missing

In Action. The likelihood now being that he's dead.' Mrs Fordham's plummy voice showed no flicker of emotion while discussing her son's possible death.

Marianne was stunned at the woman's cold matter of factness. How could she be so unfeeling? She clasped her hands together, cradling them around her swollen belly. 'I prefer to *hope* that he's still alive,' she said, fighting hard to keep the tremor she felt inside from spilling out into her voice.

Mrs Fordham gave a bitter laugh. 'Then you are even more foolish than I thought. I'll come straight to the point. Despite your *hope*,' she spoke the last word in a mocking tone, 'the reality is that the majority of airmen who go missing after their plane is hit and is last seen going down, *perish*. They die. With that in mind, my husband and I propose to take charge of our son's daughter and his new-born child.' Her eyes drifted momentarily to Marianne's belly. 'We will be able to give them a far better life and education, ones befitting of the children of someone of Alex's standing and family.'

Marianne stared at the woman in horror. 'What about me? Where do I come into your plans?'

'You don't. After you deliver your child, I'll arrange for it and the older girl to be collected and brought to live at our family home, where they will be raised in an appropriate manner.'

'By *you*?' Marianne said, fighting to keep her temper under control until she'd heard all her mother-in-law's ridiculous proposal.

'Not personally, no. I would bring Alex's old nanny out of retirement and she would answer to me.'

Marianne had heard about this nanny, a woman who was a tyrant and whom Alex had disliked. There was absolutely no way that her mother-in-law and the nanny were getting their hands on Emily and her new baby. Marianne stroked her belly as if to reassure her unborn child.

'The answer is no,' she said in a firm voice.

'It would be best for the children in the long term. Would you deny them a better home, education and upbringing?' Mrs Fordham asked in a haughty tone.

'My children will have an excellent upbringing in a loving, caring home and will be educated. Maybe not at a posh boarding school, but from what I've heard about how Alex was treated at his, then I'd much prefer them to attend local schools where I can keep a close eye on them, and where they'd come home every day.'

'But you don't even have your own house or family. What happens if you must leave here? Where will you go then? How do you plan to support yourself and the children? Working as a seamstress is a…' Mrs Fordham hesitated, her top lip curling slightly. 'A basic sort of job and with two young children to care for, how do you suppose you can do that and earn a living at the same time?'

'I think you'd better leave.' Marianne stood up. 'My answer is no, and it will stay, no.'

Mrs Fordham rose from her chair. 'You will regret that decision. I have friends in high places and the means to remove your children from you…'

The door from the hall burst open and a furious Hettie stood in the doorway looking like an annoyed and puffed-up hen.

'How dare you come here spouting such rubbish?' Hettie advanced into the room, her blue eyes blazing with fury and her cheeks rosy. She glanced at Marianne and said in a softer voice, 'Emily's with Flo and Alice in the kitchen.' Then, turning back to face Mrs Fordham, she put her hands on her hips. 'Marianne might not have a blood family to help her, but she has a family of dear friends right here at Rookery House and others in the village. And she has a home and will *always* have a home here for as long as she wants it. So you can take your ridiculous notions and clear off! Alex would be horrified at your proposal. Wanting to take children away from their mother to be brought up by some old nanny indeed! You should be ashamed of yourself.'

Mrs Fordham took a step back and seemed in retreat for a moment before recovering herself. 'Very well, I will go but…' She turned to Marianne, her blue eyes as cold as ice. 'I can assure you that you haven't heard the last of this.' With that, she swept out of the room and down the hall, banging the front door behind her as she left.

Marianne slumped down into her armchair, her body shaking with the shock of what had just happened, while Hettie went to the bay window to watch Mrs Fordham leave.

'She's gone, driven off by a chauffeur.' Hettie came back and perched on the side of the chair, putting her arm around Marianne's shoulders. 'I can't believe the cheek of the woman. How dare she suggest such a horrible thing? She wasn't even interested in talking to Emily when she had the chance. She cannot take them from you, Marianne.'

'But she said she knows people in high places,' Marianne said, her voice wavering.

'That's as maybe, but you are their mother, who loves and cares for them. There is no reason for anyone to take your children away from you,' Hettie reassured her.

'How did you know what she was saying?' Marianne asked.

Hettie gave a little chuckle. 'Because, and I hope you'll forgive me for this, I don't make a habit of it, but something told me I should, because that woman was trouble… I listened at the door.'

Marianne looked up, her eyes meeting the older woman's

for a moment before the pair of them began to laugh. 'Well, I'm glad you did. I tried my best to keep calm and listen to what she said and then you came charging in to the rescue.'

'I don't often get in a flap, but when somebody upsets someone I care about, then I let them have it. Now I think you could do with a cup of hot, sweet tea after that.' Hettie stood up. 'I won't be long.'

Marianne took hold of Hettie's hand and gave it a squeeze. 'Thank you.'

Left on her own, Marianne stared into the orange flames dancing in the fireplace. Alex being Missing In Action was bad enough, but now there was the added threat that his mother might take Emily and the baby after it was born. Hettie had reassured Marianne that couldn't happen, but was she right?

CHAPTER 30

'It sounds like most of the soldiers we've spoken to today are pleased about the Americans joining the war,' Prue said as she put a clean cup safely back into one of the compartments in a crockery drawer of the WVS canteen.

'It could help turn the tide and bring things to an end sooner than if they kept out of it,' Thea said, drying the last of the washed cups.

The sisters had been out in the mobile canteen all day doing their extra Friday shift, and were now parked up by a village station which a company of soldiers had marched to from their army camp four miles away ready to catch the train. Many of them had chatted to Thea and Prue about the latest war news as they'd waited to be served.

Events had moved on fast since Sunday when Japan had declared itself at war with Britain and the United States of America. President Roosevelt had retaliated by declaring war on Japan a few days ago. Then yesterday, Germany and Italy had announced they were at war with America too. This had been swiftly followed by America declaring war on both countries in return, joining with Britain and the other Allies in the fight against the Nazis in Europe as well as the Japanese in Asia.

'America's a lot bigger than Germany, so they're going to add a considerable might to the Allied Forces,' Prue said. 'We need all the help we can get.'

'They made a difference in the Great War. The sheer number of them was a boost to our armies who had already slogged through three long years of fighting.' Thea stowed the dried teaspoons away in a drawer. 'I met quite a few American soldiers when I was in France. They were a nice bunch. Friendly, polite and generous, but shocked by the conditions of the trenches. Some of our soldiers weren't so keen on them because the Americans got paid a lot more than the British Tommies and they splashed their money around. It made the American soldiers more popular customers than the British in the local French shops and cafes. The shopkeepers and cafe owners even put up their prices to make the most of the Americans' cash.'

'I can imagine that didn't go down well. The new boys in town becoming more popular than the men who had already been there fighting in the mud for three years.'

Thea nodded. 'That was how it was.' She looked around the well-organised canteen, checking what else there was to do before they could set off to return it to its base in Wykeham. 'I think we just need to give the surfaces a clean and sweep the floor and we're done here.'

'I'll wash the counter if you do the floor.' Prue reached for the cloth in the bowl of hot soapy water.

As Thea got to work with the small dustpan and brush, she thought back to her time in France when the Americans had arrived in the summer of 1917. The French had been delighted to see them and she recalled seeing a photograph in the newspaper of the delighted locals lining the streets of a seaside town to see the newly arrived troops parading through.

'I suppose the American soldiers will have to come here first, this time. They can't land in France with it being under German occupation.' Thea swept the small pile of crumbs she'd brushed up into the dustpan before standing up.

'We might end up serving some of them from our canteen,' Prue said. 'They'll sound like movie stars with their American accents.'

Thea gave a laugh. 'If we get any stationed around here, it will shake things up again. Be yet another change brought by the war.'

Prue tipped the bowl of water out of the open back door of the canteen on to the grass. 'There's already been plenty of changes and there will be more before it's done. They're not all bad. We've both gained a lot from doing things for the war effort. It's given us new friends and experiences. We wouldn't be doing this for a start, would we?'

Thea stowed the dustpan and brush in a cupboard, having emptied the crumbs outside for the birds to eat. 'Every cloud has a silver lining, as Hettie would say.'

'She's a wise woman.' Prue put her arm around Thea's shoulders. 'I enjoy doing this work with you. It gives us a chance to be together and talk away from the ties of home.'

Thea leaned her head against Prue's for a moment. 'I'm glad you signed up for the WVS so we could. Adding it to the many other things you do.' She smiled at her sister. 'I don't know how you manage it all, Prue.'

Her sister gave a little shrug. 'I like being busy, you know me. While there are still things that need doing for the war effort, I'll keep on doing all I can!'

CHAPTER 31

Marianne had never felt less like going to a Christmas party as she and Emily arrived at the village hall. The worry over what had happened to Alex and where he was had never left her. That, combined with the threat made by her mother-in-law to take Emily and the new baby away, weighed on Marianne's shoulders like a heavy cloak.

It had been two weeks since her mother-in-law visited Rookery House and there had been no word from her since then. Marianne suspected that a woman like Alex's mother would not back down easily and was probably just biding her time, waiting for the baby to be born. Then she would swoop in with the might of her wealth and powerful connections to try to snatch Marianne's children away from her.

Both worries made it hard for Marianne to feel much delight in the approaching festive season. She would have preferred to have stayed at Rookery House this afternoon rather than attending the Christmas party, but she didn't want to let Hettie down after all the work she'd put into organising it along with her friend, Gloria. Taking a deep breath, she braced herself and, together with Emily, walked in through the doors of the village hall, thinking that they would just stay for a short while and then go home.

Inside, the hall had been transformed from its usual plain functional space into a festive party venue. A large Christmas tree stood in the corner at the far end, its fresh pine scent filling the air. It had been beautifully dressed with colourful glass baubles that glinted as they caught the light. Newspaper chains hung in looping swathes across the ceiling and around the walls. The windows were decorated with paper snowflakes, each one unique. White cloth-covered trestle tables had been set up near the kitchen door where food and drink would be served from later.

The hall was filled with the sound of happy chattering and music from the gramophone which had been loaned by Lady Campbell-Gryce. Dancers were enjoying themselves on a makeshift dance floor at the far end. The Christmas spirit had well and truly arrived in Great Plumstead.

A tugging on her hand drew Marianne's attention to her daughter, who was pointing up at the decorations, her eyes wide with wonder.

'Look!' Emily said.

'Do you like them?' Marianne asked.

The little girl nodded, moving her arm to point at the snowflake-covered windows.

Her daughter's delight warmed Marianne's heart. Coming here this afternoon was hard for her, but it had been the right thing to do in a bid to keep everything as normal as possible for Emily. Hard as it was at times, Marianne was determined not to let the uncertainty that hung over them spoil things for her daughter.

'Let's go and have a look at the Christmas tree.' Marianne led the way to the end of the hall, keeping to the side to avoid the dance floor. They were greeted by many 'hellos', smiles and waves from villagers she knew. Everyone looked like they were enjoying themselves.

Reaching the tree, Emily stared at it, her eyes transfixed by the baubles which swung slightly, their shiny colours reflecting the light. The little girl reached out and touched the nearest one.

'That's it, nice and gently.' Marianne kept a close eye on her daughter and the glass bauble.

'You're here! I've been watching out for you to arrive,' a familiar voice said.

Marianne turned to see Hettie approaching, a warm, welcoming smile on her face.

'The hall looks beautiful,' Marianne said.

Hettie nodded as she glanced around at the decorations. 'It certainly does. Every year we have these Christmas parties, we get better at doing them.' She turned her attention to Emily. 'Have you seen the angel?'

Hettie bent down and picked the little girl up, showing her the angel sitting on the top of the tree, whose white net skirt glittered with tiny silver sequins.

'Look, Mamma!' Emily beamed as she pointed to the angel.

'She's beautiful.' Marianne returned her daughter's smile.

The record that had been playing on the gramophone when they'd arrived had come to a finish and been changed to another, this one with a jazzy toe-tapping beat.

Emily wriggled in Hettie's arms to be put down and then started jiggling and bobbing around as she often did to music on the wireless at home.

'Looks like somebody wants to join in with the dancing,' Hettie said, her eyes twinkling in amusement behind her round glasses.

'Then let's do it properly.' Marianne took hold of Emily's

hand and led her to the side of the dance floor, taking care to keep out of the way of other dancers, and the pair of them did an impromptu dance, enjoying moving to the uplifting beat of the music.

A heavily pregnant woman circling round and jigging about, hand in hand with a twenty-three-month-old, wouldn't win any prizes for style or technique, Marianne thought, but they were both having fun. The expression of joy on Emily's face filled Marianne with happiness. Right here, right now, it didn't matter what the future held, she told herself. All she needed to do was focus on the present moment. Whatever was to come, she would deal with when it happened.

Twirling around, Marianne joined in as Emily laughed with delight and let the music and motion sweep her away for a while.

CHAPTER 32

As Ned steered Evie around the dance floor, she caught a glimpse of Marianne and little Emily dancing over on the far side. The pair of them had happy smiles on their faces and looked like they were thoroughly enjoying themselves. It was a heart-warming sight. Evie had seen how Marianne's worry about what had happened to Alex weighed heavily on her. Not knowing what had become of her husband, even if he was still alive, must be hard for Marianne to bear, especially when she was soon to have their second child.

'You're looking thoughtful,' Ned said, leaning closer for a moment so his voice could be heard above the music.

'I just spotted Marianne and Emily dancing over there.' She nodded with her head towards the side of the dance floor. 'It's good to see them looking happy.'

'Is there any word of her husband?' Ned asked.

'Nothing. We're all hoping the old saying that *no news is good news* will work out for them,' Evie said. 'At least for the moment they're having fun, enjoying the music and dancing.'

'It's impossible not to feel happy with this music playing.' Ned spun Evie around, making her laugh.

Evie couldn't remember a time when she'd ever danced so much at a party. Ned had asked her to dance as soon as they'd arrived and they hadn't stopped since.

It was a sharp contrast to whenever she'd gone with Douglas to a party or occasion where there'd been dancing. He'd hated dancing and would do the minimum he possibly could get away with to be socially acceptable. Then he would abandon Evie to sit and watch for the rest of the evening. He didn't want to dance with her, but didn't want her dancing with other men, either. Evie'd had to turn down all offers to dance and been forced to sit by herself on the side of the dance floor because of her husband's wishes. It had been yet another way that Douglas had controlled and dominated her. But now she was free to dance as much as she wanted, Evie thought, her feet carrying her across the floor in the energetic two-step and she loved it!

When the record came to an end and the last notes had faded away, Evie and Ned halted, both breathing hard from their fast-paced dancing.

'Shall we take a break? I'm getting hot,' Evie said.

'Same here,' Ned agreed. 'Why don't we step outside to cool off for a few minutes, and then get a drink and something to eat? It looks like they're setting up for a tea break soon anyway.' He gestured to where Hettie, Prue and some other women were bringing plates of food and tea urns in from the kitchen and putting them out on the white cloth-covered tables.

'Good idea,' Evie agreed and led the way towards the door out of the village hall.

Once outside, she took in several deep breaths, enjoying the crisp December air, which was helping to cool her warm cheeks. There had been a frost last night and there were still patches of it remaining in the shadows. She looked up at the sky, which was a clear blue now, but which would soon start to fade as the sun sank and the long winter night descended.

'It's midwinter's day tomorrow,' she said, 'that always feels like a turning point of the year as the days will grow longer, and then spring's just around the corner.'

She turned to Ned and saw that he was watching her, his grey eyes full of tenderness. Then, without warning, he took a step towards her and kissed her softly on the lips. To her surprise, Evie found herself responding, but then her head took control of her emotions and she stepped back.

'I'm sorry I…' she began.

Ned put his hand on her arm. 'I'm sorry, I shouldn't have… but I have wanted to do that for so long.' His eyes met hers. 'I love you, Evie. I know you've been through a lot and…' He hesitated. 'Well, you might not even consider someone like me in that way. Now I've gone and told you, is there any chance at all that you would step out with me?'

Evie stared at him for a few moments before looking away, her heart pounding inside her. What should she say? What did she want? Her mind was warning her, telling her to say 'no', but her heart was telling her the opposite.

'You don't have to say anything now.' Ned's voice was gentle. 'There's no rush. Will you at least consider what I said?'

Evie found herself nodding.

'Thank you. And if you decide it's not what you want, I'll understand and hope we can still be friends,' he reassured her.

Dear sweet Ned, Evie thought, he really was the loveliest of men. 'You've caught me by surprise, but I promise I'll think about it.'

He gave her a relieved smile. 'Thank you. Now, how about

we go and get something to eat and drink? And then would you like to do some more dancing?'

'Good idea, and yes, I'd love to dance again,' Evie said, trying to keep her voice normal.

As they walked back into the hall and headed to the refreshment tables, she was grateful for some distraction. Ned's declaration had shifted something inside her. He wasn't pressuring her. It was her choice to say yes or no. But with her heart and head telling her different things, and the memory of her time with Douglas making her wary, she was conflicted. However, Ned was nothing like her late husband, Evie reminded herself. So what should she do?

CHAPTER 33

As the train pulled into Great Plumstead station with a squealing of brakes and a blast of steam that plumed in the cold air, Thea looked for Anna in the passing carriages. Coming to meet Anna at the station was always nicer than having to say goodbye to her. Thea was looking forward to having her friend home for ten days over the Christmas holidays.

Spotting Anna climbing down from a carriage near the far end of the train, Thea waved and hurried towards her.

'It's so lovely to see you.' Thea threw her arms around the young woman as she put down her suitcase. 'How are you?'

'I am well, thank you,' Anna said as Thea released her. 'I am pleased to be back here again. How are *you*?' Her brown eyes met Thea's. 'I know how hard you work.'

'I'm well, but I must admit I am looking forward to Christmas and taking things easier for a day or two.' Thea picked up Anna's case. 'Let me carry this for you. The Christmas party is on at the village hall. I wasn't sure if you'd like to go there or would rather head straight home to Rookery House?'

Anna considered for a moment and then her face broke into a smile. 'I think the Christmas party sounds good. Who will be there?'

'Most people you know in the village. Everyone from Rookery House is there. I was there earlier and it certainly looked like everyone was having a good time.'

'Then that is where I should like to go first,' Anna said in a sure voice. 'It will be the start of our Christmas holiday enjoyment.'

Thea linked her arm through Anna's and the pair of them headed off to the village hall to join in the fun.

Anna had barely taken off her coat and stowed her suitcase in the corner of the hall when she heard her name being called and moments later, she was wrapped in warm, loving arms.

'Hello, Hettie,' Anna said, returning the older woman's embrace.

From the first moment she'd met Hettie, Anna had instantly warmed to her. Hettie's caring and loving nature made her a grandmother figure to everyone who lived at Rookery House. Having lost her own Mama and leaving her Papa behind when she'd fled from Germany, to have a grandmotherly figure come into her life was an unexpected and welcome joy to Anna. Thea was like her older sister and together with all the others at Rookery House, they had become Anna's family. To be back here with them filled Anna's heart with happiness.

'Let's have a look at you.' Hettie stepped back, keeping her hands on Anna's forearms as she looked her up and down and then fixed her gaze on Anna's face. 'It's good to see you. Come on, let's get you something to eat, then you can enjoy the party. Everyone's looking forward to seeing you.'

Hettie took hold of Anna's hand and led her towards where the tables were set up with food. Getting there wasn't straightforward, as one after another people stopped to greet Anna. By the time they reached the food table, Anna felt truly welcomed back into the heart of the village. Considering she spent most of the year away at the school, it was clear that she hadn't been forgotten and was still thought of as part of the community.

After Anna had helped herself to a cup of tea, some sandwiches and one of what looked like Hettie's delicious currant buns, she felt a tap on her shoulder and turned around to see Blanche Stimpson who ran the village post office.

'Anna, how lovely to see you!' Blanche gave her a welcoming smile. 'Will you join me at my table? I'd like to catch up with you. Hear how you are.'

Anna returned her smile. 'Hello, Blanche. I will, thank you.'

As she followed Blanche to one of the small tables that had been set out around the sides of the village hall, Anna recalled her first encounter with the older woman, which had been the total opposite of today's warm greeting.

They had met soon after Anna had arrived in Great Plumstead. Like all enemy aliens, Anna was required to register at the local police station if she moved to a different address, so Thea had taken her into Wykeham to do that. It had been market day and they'd met Blanche, who'd been friendly at first until she'd heard Anna's German surname and accent. Blanche's demeanour had instantly changed and she had accused Anna of being a Nazi spy, which couldn't have been further from the truth. Back home in Germany, Anna had been reviled by the Nazis and those who supported their regime because she was Jewish. She would never have spied for them.

'You're looking thoughtful,' Blanche said as they sat down.

'I was just thinking about the first time we met.' Anna's gaze met Blanche's.

The older woman's cheeks grew pink. 'Don't remind me! I was a narrow-minded, prejudiced fool. I'm ashamed of the way I behaved towards you. I am sorry, Anna.'

'It is in the past. Prejudice comes from fear and not understanding or knowing the truth,' Anna said in a gentle tone, before taking a sip of tea.

'Thanks to Prue, you taught me and others a lot at that WI meeting. You were so brave to stand up there and tell us what you'd experienced at the hands of the Nazis in Germany. How their rules made life more and more difficult for Jewish people. I've never forgotten that and when I get fed up with this war, I remind myself that's why we need to keep fighting to stop that crazy man, Hitler.' Blanche sat back in her chair and let out a heavy sigh. 'We will defeat him!'

'I have not forgotten that it was you who helped to get me released from the camp on the Isle of Man. If you hadn't helped Thea to get an appointment at the Home Office through your niece working there, then I would probably have stayed in the camp for much longer.'

'I was glad I could do something,' Blanche said. 'Now tell me how you're getting on at the school. Are you enjoying it?'

'Yes, I am. I love to teach and the girls are mostly eager to learn. The only thing that is not so good is that it is so far away from here, but I come home in the holidays when I can. I am pleased to be here in time for the party.' Anna glanced around the hall, smiling at the villagers having fun. A jaunty tune was playing on the gramophone and the dance floor was packed with couples. She spotted Thea dancing with her brother Reuben and gave them a wave.

'It's a perfect day to come home,' Blanche agreed. 'We're all looking forward to Christmas.'

'I had never taken part in a Christmas until I came to England, but I enjoy joining in, especially at Rookery House. Thea and Hettie make it a very special, warm and joyful occasion.'

'They're like family to you now,' Blanche said.

Anna paused, her hand halfway to her mouth holding a fish-paste sandwich. 'Yes, they are. I was very lucky the day I was offered the chance to come to Rookery House.' Her gaze met Blanche's. 'And to live in Great Plumstead with the good people here. Look at how they like to have fun!' She gestured with her hand towards the party goers. 'There might be a war on, but everyone has joined together to celebrate and enjoy themselves.'

Blanche laughed. 'We certainly know how to have fun when the opportunity arises!'

CHAPTER 34

'Don't mind me saying, but if I'm not mistaken, you've been reading the same page for the past ten minutes,' Flo said, from where she lay in her bed.

Evie put her book down, turned onto her side and looked across the gap between their beds, which was lit by the golden glow from the candle burning on the nightstand. 'You're right. I can't concentrate tonight.'

Flo, who was lying facing Evie, closed her own book and gazed at her. 'Are you all right?'

Evie frowned. 'Not really. I'm not sure what to do.' She explained what had happened outside the village hall that afternoon. 'My head's telling me one thing and my heart another.'

'Do you like Ned more than just as a friend then?' Flo probed.

Evie's cheeks grew warm. 'Yes, I think I do, but...' She let out a heavy sigh. 'It doesn't mean I should do anything about it, though. I've promised myself that I will *never* get involved that way with a man again.'

'But Ned isn't anything like Douglas, is he?'

'No, quite the opposite. But even Douglas seemed nice to start with before I married him. Only then did his real character come out.' Evie pleated the top of her blanket with her fingers. 'The same could happen with Ned.'

'From what I've seen of him, he doesn't seem the sort to be like that. And he's not asking you to marry him, is he?' Flo said.

'No. But I'm scared. I do like him very much. We both love books and get on so well. The problem is, if I took a chance, and it went wrong, then I could lose a good friend.'

'Or you could take a chance and maybe you would gain a lovely man and it could lead to more in time,' Flo suggested. 'Some things are worth taking a risk for.'

Evie considered for a moment. 'I suppose they are.'

'Ned told you there's no rush, so take your time and work out what to do. Perhaps it's too soon to become more than friends. If that's the case, he would probably be happy to wait, consider you worth waiting for!' Flo reasoned.

'I need to think carefully about what I want. If I rush my decision, I could be making a big mistake. He caught me by surprise this afternoon.' Evie paused for a moment before going on. 'I am not the same innocent, unworldly girl I was when I said yes to Douglas. This time I'm wiser, more experienced and no longer afraid to say no if it's what I think is the best thing to do.'

'Good for you, Evie.' Flo gave her an encouraging smile. 'I hope whatever you decide, you'll be happy.'

Evie returned her friend's smile. 'Thank you. Being happy in life is important.'

CHAPTER 35

Christmas Eve

Rookery House was busy with preparations for Christmas. Sitting at the kitchen table, Marianne spooned home-made mincemeat into the pastry cases lining the individual compartments of a baking tray.

'The mincemeat isn't how I'd like but it's not bad, all things considered,' Hettie said as she rolled out more pastry to make the tops of the pies.

'It smells delicious,' Marianne said, breathing in the mouth-watering, warm spicy aroma of some already cooked mince pies that were cooling on the wire rack at the far end of the table. She added another spoonful of mincemeat to a pastry case. 'Despite the rationing, you've adapted the recipe brilliantly. It doesn't matter that there aren't as many raisins or currants in it, using dried plums and apples is just as tasty.'

'Not forgetting a good dash of brandy!' Hettie chuckled. 'If we can get these in the oven soon, they'll be ready for when the others return. A warm mince pie and a hot drink will be just the ticket after a walk in the cold winter air.'

'I hope the exercise will have tired the children out a bit,' Marianne said. 'George and Betty are so excited. Even though Emily doesn't understand what's happening, she's joining in with their exuberance.'

Marianne had been glad when Thea suggested taking all the children out for a walk in the woods. Thea, Prue and Rueben's sister, Lizzie, who'd arrived earlier in her car from Norwich to spend Christmas with them, had gone along with Anna to help. They would probably end up having to carry Emily part of the way as her little legs couldn't keep up with George and Betty, although she always tried hard to.

After spooning mincemeat into the last pastry case, Marianne leaned forward to pass the baking tray down the table ready to have the tops put on. A twinge in her spine made her catch her breath, and she rubbed the small of her back.

'Are you all right?' Hettie asked, a look of concern on her face.

Marianne nodded. 'I'm fine. I probably just pulled a muscle lifting Emily out of her cot this morning. The bigger I get, the harder it is to pick her up properly without twisting.' She placed her hand on her large belly. 'This gets in the way!'

Hettie fixed her with a stare. 'It could be a sign that the baby's on its way.'

Marianne shook her head. 'I didn't get a back pain like that with Emily. I'm sure it's just a pulled muscle and will soon get better.

'If you think so, then you must be careful,' Hettie said. 'The last thing you need now is to hurt your back. It might be better to ask one of us to help with lifting Emily until after the baby is born.'

The outside door into the kitchen opened and Flo stuck her head around it. 'We've got the Christmas tree. Shall we take it in through the front door?'

'Definitely! I'm not having it carried through my kitchen,' Hettie said, firmly. 'We don't want any pine needles ending up in the mince pies.'

Flo laughed. 'I'm with you on that. We'll bring it in via the front then. Reuben's brought us a smashing tree from the Hall estate,' she added before closing the door and heading off around to the front of the house.

Marianne stood up. 'I'll go and let them in.'

After opening the front door, Marianne stood to the side of the hall in the doorway of the dining room as Reuben and Flo carried the Christmas tree inside. With them came the fresh scent of pine and cold, crisp winter air. Marianne breathed it in appreciatively. Few other smells were so evocative of the festive season.

She closed the door and followed them into the sitting room where they'd positioned the beautiful, conical-shaped tree in the bay window at the front of the house. Standing upright, its roots encased in a soil-filled, large, galvanised pail, it was the perfect size.

'What do you think?' Flo asked. 'Isn't it a beauty?'

'It certainly is.' Marianne stepped towards the tree and gently touched it, its scent bringing the outdoors inside. 'Thank you, Reuben, for getting us such a beautiful tree.'

He gave a nod of his head. 'If we're going to have a tree, then it makes sense to have a good one.'

'All it needs now are the decorations,' Flo said.

'Oh, look at that!' Hettie said, bustling into the room, her cheeks flushed from the warm kitchen. 'Once the tree's inside, it always tells me Christmas is nearly here. When the others get back, we can start to put up the decorations.' She gestured towards the two cardboard boxes which Thea had brought downstairs that morning.

A tapping on the window from outside drew everyone's attention to the happy faces of the others who'd just returned from their walk.

'I'm not so sure they've used up much energy from the look of them.' Hettie threw a wry smile at Marianne. 'But it is Christmas Eve and even an old woman like me still feels the excitement! Come on, let's get hot drinks and mince pies organised for everyone and then we can start to decorate.'

After they'd all eaten some of the freshly baked mince pies and warmed themselves with a hot drink, they congregated in the sitting room ready to begin decorating.

Emily held on to Marianne's hand, the little girl's eyes fixed on the Christmas tree. Last year she'd been too small to take much notice of what was going on so this year was the first time she could take part properly. Having a tree come inside the house was obviously disconcerting for her despite the other two children's delight.

'What shall we do first?' Thea asked.

'The tree!' George and Betty chorused. 'Please.'

Thea glanced around at the adults. 'What do you think, the tree or the room first?'

'Stop teasing the children, Thea,' Lizzie scolded, a look of mock sternness on her face. 'You jolly well know we *all* want to do the tree first!'

Thea grinned. 'Just testing.' She opened the box with *Christmas tree decorations* written on the side and the children crowded round to peer in.

'Is the angel still asleep?' George asked in a hushed voice as he gently touched the top layer of white tissue paper under which they'd tucked her back in January.

'Let's see.' Thea gently peeled back the tissue paper and there lay the angel. 'She's been resting for months and is ready to sparkle on top of this year's Christmas tree. This will be her...,' she paused for a moment, 'twenty-first Christmas! I bought her back in 1920 to go on my small Christmas tree in London and she's been on each one I've had since. Remember she goes on last?'

The children nodded as Thea carefully laid the angel on a side table.

'Let's get started!' Thea said. 'Marianne, would you help Emily put the first bauble on the tree?' She held out a dark red glass bauble.

'Thank you.' Marianne gave her friend a smile as she took the bauble gently in her hand. 'Where shall we hang it, Emily? Can you find a good spot on the tree?'

Emily pointed to several places on the tree, and Marianne held the bauble up at each one to see how it looked before they finally settled on a place and hung it right at the front where it could be seen.

After that, the decoration of the tree began in earnest. Everyone took part and helped to put the different decorations on. Many of them, like the angel, had been brought from London by Thea when she'd moved here. Others had been made by George and Betty the previous year and become part of Rookery House's Christmas traditions.

Flo, Anna, Reuben, Lizzie and Thea also hung up paper chains around the room, and paper snowflakes at the windows, while Hettie decorated the mantlepiece with swathes of green ivy and red berried holly.

After a busy hour, everything was hung on the tree or

around the room and the only decoration left to place was the angel on top of the tree.

'Who put her on the tree last year?' Thea asked.

'It was me,' Betty said.

'It's George's turn this year, then.' Thea picked up the angel from the table and held it out to the little boy.

He took it, his eyes wide. 'But I can't reach.'

'You can now,' Reuben said, scooping the little boy up and holding him high enough to reach the top.

Everyone watched as George gently placed the angel on the tree, a look of concentration on his face. Then he beamed in delight as they all applauded.

'We're ready for Christmas now!' Hettie said, her blue eyes dancing with happiness. 'May it be full of joy and happiness for us all.'

CHAPTER 36

Marianne adjusted the soft covers over Emily as the little girl's breathing settled into a gentle steady rhythm. It had taken longer than usual to settle her daughter tonight as she had picked up on George and Betty's excitement. Although Emily didn't fully understand what was going on she clearly realised it was something out of the ordinary. It wasn't an everyday occurrence to hang a stocking over the far end of the cot either, Marianne thought, glancing at the thick woollen sock which Thea had loaned for Emily to hang up.

Leaning over, Marianne gently kissed Emily's cheek then silently walked to the window, pulled the blackout curtain to the side and peeped out through the crack. It was a beautiful, clear night, the sky peppered with stars twinkling against the inky blackness. Were they shining down on Alex? she wondered. Not knowing what had happened to him was hard. Marianne tried not to dwell on the what ifs and maybes, because she had no answers, but inevitably her thoughts would often turn to her husband, especially during the quiet times like now.

'Wherever you are, I'm thinking about you and hoping you're safe and well,' Marianne whispered, sending her message up into the stars. 'I love you.'

Of course, there was no reply. Marianne blinked away tears and let the blackout curtain fall into place, then closed the inner curtains. Turning to go downstairs, the pain that had been niggling in her back on and off since this morning nipped again. It wasn't because she'd lifted Emily into her cot tonight, because Thea had come up with her to do that. But if she had pulled a muscle earlier, then it would take time to heal.

After a final glance at Emily, Marianne picked up the candle holder with its burning candle and went out, closing the door quietly behind her. Out on the landing she could hear Thea's voice coming from George and Betty's bedroom, where she was reading them a bedtime story.

Making her way down to the kitchen, Marianne was looking forward to spending some time sitting by the fire listening to the wireless before she turned in for the night. Stepping into the warm room, she saw Hettie was standing by the range watching over a saucepan of milk, while Lizzie was setting out cups on the table ready.

'I'm making some cocoa, I thought we could…' Hettie began.

Marianne gasped as she felt a sudden gush of warm, wet liquid between her legs, and she looked down in shock at the puddle on the tiled floor. A sense of déjà vu hit her. The same thing had happened here in the kitchen before Emily had been born.

'I think—' Marianne began, but her words fell away as an uncomfortable cramp low in her pelvis made her wince and grab the back of a chair. Marianne remembered that pain. Her baby was coming.

Hettie was beside her in moments, putting an arm around Marianne's waist. 'It looks like your waters have gone. That back pain you had earlier was probably things getting started. We need to telephone for the midwife.'

Marianne could have gone into the maternity home a few days ago, ready for her due date, but she hadn't wanted to leave her daughter. Instead, she'd asked for the baby to be born here at Rookery House with the local midwife in attendance. That's if she got here in time. When Emily was born in the middle of heavy snow, the midwife had been out at another call, and it had been Gloria who'd delivered Marianne's first child safely into the world.

'Lizzie, go up and fetch Thea. I'll be back in a tick, Marianne,' Hettie said before dashing out of the kitchen into the hall then reappearing a few moments later. 'I've sent Flo up to read to the children in Thea's place. She'll be down in a moment and can call the midwife. Anna's fetching you some clean clothes and we'll get you comfortable. Do you want to sit down?'

'No, best to keep moving about, I think. I did that last time, and the pains aren't coming often… yet. It will be a while. There's no rush.' Marianne's voice sounded more confident than she felt.

The next few minutes passed in a whirl of activity. While Hettie quickly mopped the floor, Marianne went to the bathroom, washed the liquid from her legs and changed into a clean nightgown and her dressing gown and slippers which Anna had fetched for her. The fresh clothes made her feel better and when she returned to the kitchen, Thea was waiting with news of the midwife.

'I'm afraid like last time she's already out at a delivery, but a message has been left for her to come here as soon as she can,' Thea explained. 'So I've telephoned Gloria. Lizzie's going to go and pick her up and bring her here. You'll be in good hands.'

Marianne nodded. 'Thank you.' Gloria had been wonderful when Emily was born. A mother of six, Gloria had plenty of experience of childbirth herself as well as helping to deliver many babies back in London. Her calmness and knowledge had carried Marianne through the last time. Knowing she'd have her friend by her side again reassured Marianne, as she felt another pain beginning to build.

'We'll get a fire lit in your bedroom so it's nice and warm in there for when the baby arrives,' Thea said.

'What about Emily?' Marianne managed, as the pain eased away.

'We'll move her and the cot into my room,' Hettie said. 'Flo and Anna,' she directed her question at the two young women who'd come into the kitchen, 'can you help Thea do that when she goes up to light the fire?'

They both nodded. The pair of them looked quite worried, Marianne thought, as she would have been faced with a woman in labour before she'd had a child of her own.

By the time Lizzie returned with Gloria, bringing in with them the scent of cold, frosty night air, Marianne had taken to pacing around the kitchen when her pains came. She still wasn't near giving birth, but things were moving along as the contractions were slowly growing in intensity and frequency.

'Hello, ducks!' Gloria strode over to Marianne in her high heeled peep-toed shoes and embraced her. 'You're planning on 'aving a Christmas baby, then?'

'It looks like it. I'm sorry to drag you out on Christmas Eve,' Marianne said. 'Thank you for coming.'

'I'm glad to 'elp.' Gloria rubbed Marianne's back.

'What about Dora?' Marianne asked.

'Oh, she's fine. Tucked up fast asleep with Sylvia happily looking after her,' Gloria replied. 'Now, let's see how far apart your pains are coming, shall we? I'll time it from the next one.'

Marianne lost all track of time for the next few hours. She spent a lot of them pacing back and forth in the kitchen, watched over by a patient and supportive Gloria. The others came and went from the room, not wanting to crowd her. A little after eleven o'clock, Gloria decided it was time for Marianne to move up to her bedroom where the baby would be born. Hettie and Thea went with them as there was still no sign of the midwife.

The warm bedroom, lit by the soft golden glow from the candles and the fire burning in the grate, felt like a welcoming cocoon to Marianne. It was the perfect place for her baby to be born. She became lost in her own world, consumed by the waves of pain and immense relief each time they passed. She was vaguely aware of Lizzie coming into the room with hot water and towels.

As her labour progressed, the memories of how it had been when Emily was born came back to her. Things that she'd forgotten immediately afterwards, and never remembered until now. They helped to calm her, helped her understand and accept what was happening as her body took over doing its job to deliver the baby.

'You're doing really well, ducks.' Gloria rubbed the small of Marianne's back. 'It won't be long before your little one arrives. Do you want to change position? Or lie down?'

Marianne shook her head. Whenever she tried lying down, it felt worse. 'Stay standing,' she said, wincing as another wave of pain started to build.

'Relax and breath through the contraction,' Gloria said in a soft voice.

'It's coming!' Marianne could feel the baby moving downwards. She held on tight to the end of her iron bedstead, leaning towards it, with Hettie and Thea on each side of her, their hands on her shoulders.

'Keep going,' Hettie encouraged her. 'You're doing so well.'

Marianne gasped as a burning sensation burst between her legs.

'Pant! Don't push,' Gloria ordered, kneeling on the floor behind Marianne, ready to catch the baby. 'I can see the head.'

Marianne was aware that Hettie and Thea were panting along with her, and if she wasn't in so much agony, she would have laughed at what must be a funny sight. Then another pain hit her.

'Push now, but gently!' Gloria warned her.

Marianne did as she was told, fighting the urge to squeeze as hard as she could. She focused her energy and mind on doing the right thing to get her baby born safely.

'The head's out! Well done. You're nearly there. Just one more push when the next pain comes. You can do it,' Gloria encouraged her.

As soon as another pain hit, Marianne pushed, felt her baby slither out and a heard a squeal of delight from Gloria, quickly followed by a sharp gusty wail from the baby. 'You've got a lovely little girl.'

Tears filled Marianne's eyes as she turned to see her new daughter. Filled with a rush of euphoria, the pains of the last few hours were forgotten as she saw her beautiful baby for the first time.

'Have you seen the clock?' Thea said, her voice wavering with emotion. 'It's a quarter past midnight. It's Christmas Day.'

'You have a Christmas baby!' Gloria added, quickly clamping and cutting the cord before wrapping the little girl in a warm towel, which Lizzie held out to her. 'The best present of all.'

'Do you have a name for her?' Hettie asked.

'Beatrice. Alex said if we had another daughter, that's what he'd like to call her, so that's her name.' Marianne reached out and took her daughter in her arms and gently stroked her baby's cheek with her finger. 'Hello, Beatrice.'

CHAPTER 37

Christmas Day

Thea hummed the tune of *Away in a Manger* to herself as she milked Primrose. She often sang or hummed as she did the milking, as she'd noticed that the cow let her milk down more easily if there was some musical accompaniment. It was lovely to sit and sing or hum along as she worked. With today being Christmas Day, carols seemed appropriate and none more so than this one Thea thought, her hands working in a steady rhythm.

It might be Christmas Day, but as far as the animals that lived at Rookery House were concerned, it was like any other. They all had to be fed and cared for, the work of looking after them couldn't stop because of what day it was. The same applied to Evie, who'd gone to do her shift at the hospital as usual this morning, although there would be some celebrations there to mark the day.

While Thea was in here milking Primrose, Flo was taking

care of the pigs, rabbits and chickens, making sure they had plenty of food and water. There had been a sharp frost overnight and it had snowed during the early hours, blanketing the world in several inches of white. The clouds had cleared and it had dawned bright and fine, with a clear blue sky arching overhead, but there was a cold nip in the air as the temperature had remained below freezing.

When she'd finished the milking, Thea put the pail of milk safely to the side, then checked that Primrose still had plenty of hay in the hayrack for her to eat and a full pail of water to drink. With the grass outside covered in snow, the cow would be staying inside and eating hay from Rookery House's first crop, which they'd dried and harvested back in June. The sweet smell of it filling the air reminded Thea of those hot summer days when they'd spent hours turning it and bringing it in by hand just in time before a thunderstorm broke. It had been a new venture for her, another change at Rookery House, and well worth all the effort and hard work.

As she stroked under Primrose's chin, Thea reflected on how the past few hours had brought another change, with the arrival of baby Beatrice. It had been an anxious time hoping nothing would go wrong, but thankfully, with Gloria's help, Marianne had given birth to a beautiful baby girl, and all was well. Thea had peeped in at them before she'd come out to do the milking and both mother and the baby were sleeping, no doubt exhausted from the birth.

Thea was tired this morning. It had been the early hours before she had gone to bed, and it had only seemed like five minutes later when she'd been woken by two visitors to her room a little after six o'clock. George and Betty had brought their stockings with them, which had been filled by Father Christmas in the night, and were eager to see what was inside.

Pushing her tiredness to the side, Thea had welcomed them in and loved watching their joy at discovering their gifts.

'I can catch up on some sleep tonight,' she said, giving Primrose a final pat. 'I'll be out to check on you later.'

Leaving the cow to carry on munching the hay, Thea picked up the pail of milk and headed indoors, ready for some breakfast.

Thea was in the scullery washing out the pail, having transferred the milk into jugs to be kept in the cool of the pantry, when the outside door opened and Flo came in with a blast of icy air.

'Are the animals all right?' Thea asked.

'Yes, they're all fine.' Flo kicked off her rubber boots and stood them tidily beside the other pairs lined up against the scullery wall near the door. 'Although I don't think the pigs know quite what to make of the snow. It's the first they've seen.' Flo took off her coat, scarf and hat and hung them on one of the pegs on the wall above the boots. 'They tried eating it when I let them out into their yard and when I left them they were playing about shovelling it around with their noses!'

Thea laughed. 'Not surprising with those two. They're such a playful pair.'

'I cleared a patch of snow near the hen coop so those that want to go out can. Some of them kept indoors in the coop. Don't blame them as their feet get so cold.' Flo came over to the sink and washed her hands as Thea had finished washing the pail and had left it upside down on the draining board. 'I put the rabbits' food in their hutches for them so if they don't want to venture out into their snowy runs, they don't have to. Is Primrose all right?'

'Yes, she's fine. She had a quick look outside, turned her

nose up at the snow and went back to eating the hay inside,' Thea said. 'Now it's our turn to eat before we relax and enjoy the day until we need to go out and do it all over again!'

It was a little after two o'clock on Christmas afternoon when Thea, Reuben, Anna, Flo and Lizzie took the children outside for some fresh air and exercise. After the excitement of opening their gifts, followed by a delicious meal, Thea thought time spent playing in the snow would be good for them *all*, not just for the children. The washing up and clearing up had been done and it hadn't taken long with many helping hands. After cooking a magnificent meal, Hettie had gone to doze in an armchair by the fire in the sitting room with Marianne and baby Beatrice for company.

'Shall I get the sledge out?' Reuben asked as his dog Bess bounded along beside him in the snow, her breath pluming in the cold, crisp air.

'Yes please,' George said, his face alight with excitement. The little boy, like everyone else, was well wrapped up in a warm coat, hat and scarf and his feet kept dry in rubber boots.

'Can Emily have a go this time?' Betty asked as Reuben headed off to one of the sheds to fetch the sledge. 'She was too young before.'

Emily, who was holding onto Betty's hand, gave a wide smile at the sound of her name.

'I think so, if she has a turn with you and you can hold on tight to her,' Thea said. When they'd had snow back in January, Emily had been too small and hadn't even been walking. Now the little girl was on her feet and joined in playing with Betty and George as much as she could.

'Let's build a snowman.' Lizzie picked up a handful of snow and shaped it into a ball. Then she put it on the ground and started rolling it along, the snowball growing quickly as it gathered more snow around it with each turn.

'I'll do the head.' Flo started another ball, rolling it along like Lizzie.

'I shall find some things for the eyes and nose,' Anna said, heading off to look for something suitable.

'Will you pull us on the sledge, Auntie Thea, please?' George asked, slipping his mittened hand into Thea's. 'But not too fast. We don't want Emily to fall off.'

Thea smiled down at the little boy. 'Of course, and I promise I'll take it slowly.'

George nodded, his face serious. He'd been surprised and fascinated to see baby Beatrice this morning. Thea had taken him and Betty up to Marianne's room to visit the baby after breakfast. Hettie had already taken Emily in earlier to meet her new sister and the little girl had been proud to show Beatrice to George and Betty.

'Who's having a ride first?' Reuben asked, returning with the wooden sledge.

'George, Betty and Emily are all going together, with me pulling,' Thea informed her brother. 'George, if you sit at the front, Emily can go in the middle and Betty, you sit behind and hold on tight to her. Reuben, will you walk behind?'

Reuben nodded. 'Climb aboard!' He helped the children settle themselves into place on the sledge.

Once they were seated and ready, Thea took hold of the rope. 'Hold on tight!' She began to pull it slowly and steadily, taking frequent glances over her shoulder to make sure they were safe. The wide smiles on their faces and giggles of delight coming from them were a joy to see.

By the time Thea and Reuben had taken the children on a tour around Rookery House gardens and the edge of Five

Acre Field and back to where they'd started, Flo, Anna and Lizzie were putting the finishing touches to their snowman.

'You haven't lost the touch, Lizzie,' Thea said to her youngest sister. 'Or the joy of making a snowman.'

Lizzie laughed, her gaze meeting Thea's. 'You're never too old to enjoy making a snowman. Or to have a snowball fight, either.' She scooped up a handful of snow and threw it at Thea, who stepped to one side so it hit Reuben's chest.

Without saying anything he grabbed a handful and retaliated, sending it flying back at Lizzie. Soon everyone was joining in, even little Emily, who just threw handfuls of snow in the air laughing.

Five minutes later, red-cheeked and breathless from running around, they all came to a halt laughing.

'I am so glad I came home for the Christmas holiday,' Anna said. 'I haven't played in the snow for such a long time.'

'Me neither,' Lizzie said. 'My fingers and toes have gone numb though, so I think it's time I went in.'

'We should all go in,' Thea added. 'We can warm up by the fire and have some mince pies. There's plenty left.'

As they headed inside, everyone glowing and happy from playing in the snow, Thea realised that this was the third Christmas of the war. At least for today, they had pushed that to the side and enjoyed time together as family and friends. Christmas Day 1941 was turning out to be a special one indeed!

CHAPTER 38

Evie loved how the scent of Christmas had come to Great Plumstead Hall Hospital. Pushing a trolley loaded with covered plates of the festive dinner for the bed-bound patients, she passed by the large Christmas tree that stood in the hall. Its fresh, pine fragrance filled the air and was so evocative of the season. The estate grown tree had been brought in two days ago and Lady Campbell-Gryce, assisted by mobile patients, had decorated it with an assortment of beautiful decorations that twinkled prettily as they caught the light.

Yesterday evening, they'd sung carols around the tree. Mrs Platten, the Quartermaster, had provided the musical accompaniment on the piano which had been pushed into the hall for the occasion. Patients and hospital staff had been joined by workers from the gardens and estate grounds. Together, their combined singing of the age-old songs had made Evie's skin tingle and her heart soar. It had been a wonderful start to the celebrations.

Now it was Christmas Day and while essential jobs still

had to be carried out, all the staff were doing their best to make things special for their patients. The Christmas dinner Evie was delivering to the wards was just one of the extras to celebrate the day and more were planned for later.

Arriving at Library Ward, Evie was surprised to find Ned sitting on a chair next to Private Chambers' bed, the pair of them chatting away.

The rattling sound of the trolley must have caught Ned's attention as he looked around and, on seeing her, his face broke into a wide smile. 'Merry Christmas, Evie… I mean Nurse Jones!'

'Merry Christmas to you, Mr Blythe,' Evie replied, returning his smile. 'What are you doing in here?'

'I'm volunteering for the day,' Ned said. 'Matron asked me last night if I'd like to come in and help today. She's given me the job of helping Robbie… Private Chambers here, with his Christmas dinner.'

'I was going to…' Evie began but halted, thinking that if Matron Reed wanted Ned to feed Private Chambers his meal, then it would be best not to question her order. 'Well, if you're sure.'

Ned nodded. 'Don't worry, I know how to do it properly. Remember, I was on the receiving end while my eyes were bandaged up. Imagine the mess I'd have got into eating soup if someone hadn't helped me. I won't go too quick or too slow.'

'Here you are then.' Evie took the cover off the plate and passed it to Ned along with the cutlery. 'Cook has done a wonderful job. The meat comes from cockerels reared on the estate, fresh vegetables from the garden, there are batter puddings, chestnut stuffing and plenty of gravy.'

Private Chambers gave an appreciative sniff. 'It smells good and is making my mouth water. When are you both having yours?'

'A bit later, once all the patients have had theirs. The mobile men are eating in the dining room now. I must go and deliver the rest of these meals while they're still hot.' She gestured towards the other covered plates on the trolley. 'Enjoy!'

Leaving Ned cutting the food ready to feed Private Chambers, Evie pushed the trolley out of the ward and headed off to Dining Room Ward to deliver the Christmas dinners to more hungry patients.

On her way back to the kitchen a short while later, she paused briefly by the door of Library Ward and peeped in. Ned and Private Chambers were chatting and laughing between mouthfuls. She watched as her friend carefully fed the young soldier. Ned's own experience of needing help to eat when he was a patient had clearly prepared him well to do a good job. The care and patience Ned showed warmed Evie's heart. He didn't have to be here today. He could have been spending his day off at home relaxing, but instead Ned had chosen to spend time helping at the hospital. A voice in her head pointed out that Douglas would never have dreamed of doing something like this. He'd rarely helped anyone except himself.

After a fun afternoon with staff, patients and volunteers playing parlour games, followed by a delicious tea, everyone was feeling happy and relaxed. Evie and Delia were going around collecting up the empty plates and cups to take back to the kitchen, stacking them on a trolley.

'Can I tell you something?' Delia asked. 'I have some news.'

'Of course, let's finish in here first and then you can tell me on the way to the kitchen. It will be a bit quieter,' Evie suggested, looking around the Recreation Room, which was noisy with chatter and laughter.

A short while later, as they set off for the kitchen, with the trolley loaded with rattling crockery, Evie sensed Delia was bursting with her news.

'What have you got to tell me?' she asked.

'I'm leaving!' Delia announced.

Evie halted, pulling the trolley to a standstill, and looking her friend straight in the eye. 'But why? You've worked so hard. Matron is gradually letting you do more with the patients. I know it's been frustratingly slow for you, but…'

'I'm not the right sort of person to be a nurse,' Delia cut in. 'I've tried and I do like the *idea* of it, but sadly, practically speaking, I'm just not suited to the role. I can't cope with dressings being changed and I much prefer to talk to a patient than do anything else.'

'But you'll get used to doing dressings, the more you see and do. It's a shock to everyone to start with, but you will learn to manage,' Evie said in an encouraging voice.

Delia shook her head. 'I don't think I *want* to get used to them, to be honest. I've decided I'm going to join the Wrens instead. Lady Campbell-Gryce has been telling me about her daughter Cecilia, who's in the Wrens and she's having a marvellous time. And…' Delia giggled. 'They do have a rather smashing uniform!'

'I suppose they do. It's much smarter than ours.' Evie looked down at her own blue dress and white apron. 'And they don't have to wear a ridiculous veil, either.'

'There are all sorts of jobs you can do in the Wrens,' Delia said, her voice full of enthusiasm as they headed for the kitchen once more. 'Cecilia's a driver and that sounds fun. I could do that.'

'If you're not happy being a VAD, then it's best to move on

to something else,' Evie acknowledged. 'I admire you for sticking it out for as long as you have, and for being brave enough to admit you know it's not the right thing for you.' Evie glanced at Delia. 'I hope you'll find a job that suits you and that you love doing in the Wrens.'

'Thank you. You have been so kind and encouraging to me right from my first day here when I was working in the sluice.' Delia gave a mock shudder. 'That is one job I will *definitely not miss*! And you've saved me from several tickings off from Matron too.'

'When are you leaving?' Evie asked, manoeuvring the trolley through a door leading into the long corridor in the servants' part of the hall.

'In a few days' time. I've told Lady Campbell-Gryce and she's going to break the news to Matron Reed. Not that I think she will be sad to see me go.' Delia giggled. 'She'll probably be relieved!'

'Matron's seen how hard you've worked and that counts for a lot with her,' Evie said. 'We'll miss you, Delia.'

Coming back into the wide entrance hall after delivering the used tea things to the kitchen, Evie was surprised at the sight that met them. The black and white tiled hall had been turned into an impromptu dance floor, with couples moving around to toe-tapping music blasting out of the gramophone.

'There you are,' Hazel said, spotting Evie and Delia and hurrying over.

'What's going on?' Evie asked, watching the dancers, who included a mixture of staff, volunteers and mobile patients. Even Matron was dancing, doing a passable foxtrot with Mr White, the head gardener.

'Matron had the gramophone brought through from the

Recreation Room and set about organising a dance,' Hazel said. 'It's most unlike her. I wonder if she's been at the sherry this afternoon?'

'Or maybe it's just the Christmas spirit that's made her happy,' Evie suggested with a grin. 'Or both!'

As the record finished and the music faded away, Matron noticed them standing together and came striding over, tugging Mr White behind her.

'Come along, nurses. Young girls like you should be dancing, not hanging around the edges like wallflowers!' she said in her soft Scottish voice, her cheeks flushed from dancing. 'There are men without partners. Nurse Jones, Mr Blythe hasn't had a dance yet,' Matron said pointedly, giving a small nod of her head towards the door of the Library Ward.

Evie looked over and saw Ned standing beside Private Chambers' bed, which he must have pushed to the doorway so the young soldier could watch what was going on even if he couldn't join in the dancing. Without waiting for an answer, Matron grabbed hold of Mr White again with both hands and, as the next record began, swept him away.

'Best do as Matron says,' Hazel said. 'Come on, Delia, there are a couple of patients over there who look like they would like to dance. Evie's going to be dancing with Mr Blythe, aren't you?' She raised her eyebrows, her eyes twinkling with mischief.

'If that's what Matron wants, then I'd better,' Evie agreed. She watched for a moment as her friends went to find partners and were soon part of the throng moving around the dance floor.

Evie recalled the last time she'd danced with Ned at the village Christmas party and what had happened outside. She had not forgotten what he'd asked her and had slowly been thinking it over, but she still hadn't given him an answer. True to his word, Ned had not pushed her to make up her mind and tell him yes or no. What should she do? Evie mused. Should she take a risk and say yes?

Sometimes in life things worked out, and sometimes they didn't. Look at Delia, Evie thought. She had so desperately wanted to be a nurse and had tried hard to make it work, but Delia was brave enough to recognise that it wasn't the right thing for her. When she'd joined the hospital back in October, Delia hadn't known how it would turn out, but she'd at least tried. There was no shame in admitting it hadn't worked out as she'd hoped, and it was best to move on to try something else. Every choice made in life was a risk, Evie realised. If the fear of what might go wrong stopped her from even trying, then it was a great pity, because she might just miss out on something that had the potential to be wonderful, even life changing.

Lifting her chin, Evie took a deep breath and made her way over to Ned.

'Would you like to dance?' Evie held out her hand to him with an encouraging smile on her face.

Ned glanced at Private Chambers, who nodded and winked at him.

'Don't keep the lady waiting,' Private Chambers urged him.

Ned bowed his head to her. 'I would be delighted, thank you.'

She took hold of his warm hand in hers and they walked to the edge of the dance floor and joined in.

They both spoke at the same time.

'I hope…'

'My…'

'You first.' Ned looked at her, their eyes meeting.

'My answer is yes,' Evie said.

Ned frowned and then his forehead cleared as he realised

what she was saying yes to. 'Is that a yes, you'd like to step out with me?'

Evie nodded. 'It is. I wasn't sure because of what happened before… but you're different. I want to try because I think we could have something special together.'

'Thank you for believing in me and for taking a chance on me.' He looked quite overcome.

Evie realised they'd stopped dancing in the middle of the dance floor, other couples moving around them. Before she could say anything, Ned kissed her gently on the lips.

'Nurse Jones!' Matron's voice cut through the music and they sprang apart, turning to see Matron staring at them, a smile tugging at the corners of her lips as she danced slowly past with Mr White. Her eyes flicked upwards for a moment and she raised an eyebrow. 'I'll pretend I didn't see that happen while you're on duty,' she said in a voice laced with mirth, then increased her pace and dragged Mr White off again into the throng of dancers.

Evie and Ned glanced up and saw there was a bunch of green mistletoe, dotted with plump white berries, dangling from the chandelier above their heads. They burst out laughing and as they started to dance again, Evie felt happy and light. She didn't know what the future held with Ned, but she was going to enjoy finding out. One thing for sure was he was a man worth taking a chance on.

CHAPTER 39

2nd January 1942

Marianne stroked Beatrice's soft cheek as she watched her feeding. She'd brought her daughter into the sitting room for her feed, the warmth and quiet in here more settled than the busy kitchen. Lit by the yellow glow of the candlelight and flames flickering in the fireplace, it felt cosy and relaxing and gave Marianne a chance to think.

Since Beatrice's birth on Christmas Day, the baby girl had given a much-needed boost to Marianne, sharpening her determination for the future. She'd promised herself that whatever lay ahead for them, she would do her utmost to look after and provide for her children. She didn't know if she would ever see Alex again. She dearly hoped she would someday, and he could meet his new daughter, but until that happened, if it happened, then Marianne had to be strong. Her little girls needed her and she couldn't let them down.

It was hard to believe that she now had *two* children, both born here at Rookery House. Emily had taken to her new role as a big sister with great pride, probably through having seen Betty in action looking out for George. Emily was now in the kitchen doing some drawing at the table alongside George and Betty before they all had their evening meal at five o'clock. They were being watched over by Thea and Flo, who'd come in from working outside as the January days were so short. Hettie was finishing the cooking.

The telephone began to ring out in the hall and Marianne heard the kitchen door open and then Thea's voice as she answered it. She couldn't hear what her friend was saying. Perhaps she was being called to do an extra shift for the WVS as sometimes happened.

Turning her attention to the fireplace, Marianne recalled how her grandmother used to tell her to look out for pictures in the flames. Looking at them now, Marianne couldn't see any, just the flickering colours of gold, orange and yellow.

The door of the sitting room opened and Thea came in. She closed it quietly behind her before coming over to sit down in the armchair opposite Marianne.

'I have some news!' Thea's eyes were alight with happiness. 'That was a telegram over the phone from the War Office. Alex is a Prisoner of War! He's alive, Marianne. He's alive.' Thea leaned forwards, took hold of Marianne's free hand and squeezed it.

Marianne stared at her for a few moments. 'Can you say that again?'

Thea repeated what she'd said and Marianne let the words sink in. Alex was alive and a Prisoner of War. He'd survived!

She gasped as her eyes filled with tears of relief and joy. She felt light, as if a heavy pressure had been lifted from her. In the six weeks since she had received that terrible telegram telling her that her husband was Missing In Action, she'd gone through a whole raft of emotions, imagined so many scenarios of what might have happened to him. She'd hoped, despaired, cried and even feared losing her children to her mother-in-law.

'That's wonderful. He's safe. No more flying on ops for him. Alex can wait out the war and then he will come home.' She took hold of Beatrice's hand, the baby girl curling her fingers around Marianne's. 'Your daddy will be coming home to us someday.'

'The telegram said more information will be communicated to you in a letter,' Thea added.

Marianne nodded. 'I'll need to find out where Alex is so I can write to him. Let him know he has another daughter. Will you go and tell the others for me? I need to take it in while Beatrice finishes feeding.'

'They'll be delighted.' Thea gave her a beaming smile. 'I'm so pleased for you and the girls.'

After Thea had returned to the kitchen to spread the news, Marianne closed her eyes and let the knowledge that Alex was alive settle inside her. She'd been right to keep hoping, to not give up. Her mother-in-law had been wrong and she could have no claim on her grandchildren now. She didn't even know about Beatrice's birth. Marianne sighed. For the first time in a long while she felt safe and at peace.

It was a little past midnight and Marianne had just settled Beatrice back in her crib after a night feed. Emily was sound asleep, her thumb in her mouth and her rag doll tucked under one arm. Despite the late hour, Marianne didn't feel sleepy. The news about Alex had buoyed her up and filled her with energy. She wandered over to the window, pulled a curtain to the side and then opened a small gap in the blackout curtains and looked out over the back garden of Rookery House. It was bathed in the pale light from the full moon, turning the usual shades of the day into a monochrome world.

Now Alex was no longer flying up there on ops, Marianne could look upon the full moon in a kindlier way. Instead of regarding it as a bomber's moon, which put her husband in more danger, she could see it as the beautiful celestial orb that it had always been. She wondered if it was a clear sky over where Alex was. Could he see it shining down on him? Were they both looking up at the moon right now, linked together but unable to see each other?

Marianne smiled. She would tell him when she wrote to him to look at the full moon as she did. It would feel like a connection, no matter how distant.

At teatime, Hettie had told her about the Red Cross's work linking POWs and their families and how they sent out parcels to the prisoners. Apparently, prisoners' loved ones could do the same through their network. Marianne couldn't go and visit Alex but there was a lot she could do to help him from here. She was keen to get started and would find out all she could from the local Red Cross. It filled her full of optimism and joy that she'd be able to do something at last. Alex would know that she still cared and was here looking out for him until he came home.

The new year had barely started but 1942 was turning into a better one for her than the last two months of the old year had been. Marianne could now look towards the future when the war would finally be over and Alex would come home. She had no idea how long that might take, but however many months or years it was, she and their daughters would be here waiting for him.

Dear Reader,

I hope you enjoyed catching up with Marianne and Evie again as well as spending time with Thea and Hettie at Rookery House, along with other residents of Great Plumstead. It was a delight for me to bring Violet Steele to stay too. Some of you would have known her from my *East End Angels* series, where she firmly but kindly keeps her team at Ambulance Station 75 out of mischief!

I love hearing from readers – it's one of the greatest joys of being a writer – so please do get in touch via:

Facebook: **Rosie Hendry Books** or join my private readers group - **Rosie Hendry's Reader Group**
Twitter: @hendry_rosie
Instagram: rosiehendryauthor
Website: **www.rosiehendry.com**

You can sign up to get my monthly newsletter delivered straight to your inbox, with all the latest on my writing life, exclusive looks behind the scenes of my work, and reader competitions.

If you have the time and would like to share your thoughts about this book, do please leave a review. I read and appreciate each one as it's wonderful to hear what you think. Reviews also encourage other readers to try my books.

With warmest wishes,

Rosie

IF YOU ENJOYED A CHRISTMAS BABY AT ROOKERY HOUSE...

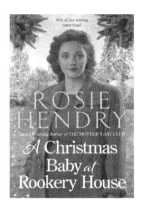

It would be wonderful if you could spare a few minutes to leave a star rating, or write a review, at the retailer where you bought this book.

Reviews don't need to be long – a sentence or two is absolutely fine. They make a huge difference to authors, helping us know what readers think of our books and what they particularly enjoy. Reviews also help other readers discover new books to try for themselves.

You might also tell family and friends you think would enjoy this book.

Thank you!

HEAR MORE FROM ROSIE

Want to keep up to date with Rosie's latest releases?

Sign up to receive her monthly newsletter at her website.
www.rosiehendry.com

Subscribers get Rosie's newsletter delivered to their inbox and are always the first to know about the latest books, as well as getting exclusive behind the scenes news, plus reader competitions.

You can unsubscribe at any time and your email will never be shared with anyone else.

Have you met the East End Angels?

Winnie, Frankie and Bella are brave ambulance crew who rescue casualties of the London Blitz.

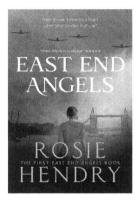

BOOK 1 - USA and Canada edition

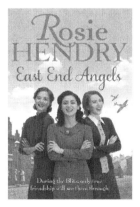

BOOK 1 - UK and rest of world English edition

Available in ebook, paperback and audiobook.

ACKNOWLEDGMENTS

Many people have helped me with my research into wartime Norfolk — a big thank you to Reepham Archive and Aylsham Heritage Centre and Archives, Norfolk Library Service for supplying many research books, and the Imperial War Museum in London for access to recorded oral histories and documents.

My mum patiently answered my many questions about life in rural Norfolk in the Second World War — thank you.

Thanks to the fantastic team who help me create the books — editor, Catriona Robb, cover designer, Andrew Brown, photographer, Gordon Crabb and proof reader, Isobel Bedford.

My fellow writers are a great support and I appreciate their friendship, company, wise words and listening ears. Thank you especially to the Strictly Saga authors and my dear friends in the RNA's Norfolk and Suffolk Chapter and especially the Famous Five!

Finally, thank you to David, who supports me in all I do.

ALSO BY ROSIE HENDRY

East End Angels novels

East End Angels

Secrets of the East End Angels

Christmas with the East End Angels

Victory for the East End Angels

Rookery House novels

The Mother's Day Club

The Mother's Day Victory

A Wartime Welcome at Rookery House

Digging for Victory at Rookery House

A Christmas Baby at Rookery House

Rookery House novella

A Wartime Christmas at Rookery House

Standalone novel

Secrets and Promises

Standalone novellas

A Home from Home

Love on a Scottish Island

Short story collection

A Pocketful of Stories

Rosie Hendry lived and worked in the USA before settling back in her home county of Norfolk, England, where she lives in a village by the sea with her family. She likes walking in nature, reading (of course) and growing all sorts of produce and flowers in her garden — especially roses.

Rosie writes stories from the heart that are inspired by historical records, where gems of social history are often to be found. Her interest in the WWII era was sparked by her father's many tales of growing up at that time.

Rosie is the winner of the 2022 Romantic Novelists' Association (RNA) award for historical romantic sagas, with *The Mother's Day Club,* the first of her series set during wartime at Rookery House. Her novels set in the London Blitz, the *East End Angels* series, have been described as 'Historical fiction at its very best!'.

To find out more visit **www.rosiehendry.com**

Printed in Great Britain
by Amazon